"How do you do, ma'am. Name's Ben Tasker . . . "

He watched her shoulders wilt and her whole body begin to quiver. Obviously she was badly frightened.

"I mean you no harm. It's just that we'll be traveling together for quite a time, and you can't go about hiding like this the entire way to Indiana."

Still, she said nothing. Well, he could wait her out. She had to be near cooking inside that cape of hers. This whole affair reminded him of the way Indians smoked out their prey by setting fire to a cabin. When the hapless victims could stand the heat no longer, they were easy pickings.

At last she was forced to abandon the cape. She kept the left side of her face completely covered, however. But when he viewed the right side for the first time, he had to stifle a gasp. She was the most beautiful woman he had ever seen!

The one eye he could see was blue. No, more a blue-green—the color of the sea in the shallows. It was large and framed with long, thick lashes that lay on her cheek like a smudge of soot as she shut her eyes against his astonished stare.

Before she closed them though, he had read the message. The lost seeking look of a trapped animal wasn't reserved for those with four legs. *Poor little creature.*

DIVIDE THE JOY

Maryn Langer

Serenade/Saga
BOOKS

of the Zondervan Publishing House
Grand Rapids, Michigan

A Note From The Author:
I love to hear from my readers! You may correspond with me by writing:

Maryn Langer
1415 Lake Drive, S.E.
Grand Rapids, MI 49506

DIVIDE THE JOY
Copyright © 1986 by Maryn Langer

Serenade/Saga is an imprint of Zondervan Publishing House,
1415 Lake Drive, S.E., Grand Rapids, Michigan 49506.

ISBN 0-310-47332-2

Printed in the United States of America

86 87 88 89 90 91 92 / 10 9 8 7 6 5 4 3 2 1

To Susan Anderson and Ann Harding
for sharing their time and talent,
for being special friends,
for praising God with every act.

Grief can take care of itself, but to get the full value of a joy you must have somebody to divide it with.

Mark Twain

CHAPTER 1

1820

IN A SECLUDED PART of the yard obscured by dog-
wood trees, Mercy Wheeler sat on a small white
bench under an ancient spreading beech. Unobserved,
she watched her brother Daniel Wheeler and his wife
Norah standing in the late April afternoon to greet
their neighbors.

"Thank you so much for your generosity," Norah's
cordial words rang out over the lawn as another guest
handed her a large basket. Norah peeked inside.
"Your fried chicken and freshly baked bread will
serve us well on our journey."

The hams, boiled eggs, chicken, plus uncounted
pies and cakes would save the Wheelers from having
to cook over an open fire during the first days of their
journey.

"Just the Shenandoah Valley way of wishing a
family well," the woman answered.

A deep voice rumbled, "So you're a goin' west to
Indiany?"

"That's right," Daniel answered. "Figure to homestead some of the best land to be had."

"Wish I could get my missus uprooted, but she's got her tap root clear to China. Nothin'll budge this woman but Gabriel. You're a lucky man, Daniel, to have such an obligin' lady." He softened his words by putting a protective arm about his wife's shoulders. "Wouldn't trade her fer all the state of Indiany though!"

If there were any doubts remaining in his wife's mind, Mercy thought, the fond look he had just bestowed on her would surely remove them.

Norah and Daniel beamed a tender smile at each other, and the other woman curled into the embracing arm of her husband. Mercy sighed. Did these women have any idea how fortunate they were to have loving men, who'd fight charging bears with a club to protect them? Mercy, the cold lump in her heart growing larger by the minute, allowed her eyes to roam over the farewell gathering, lingering on other couples. The young ones a-courting, stood apart, awkward, unsure, trying to learn of each other. Those now stooped and wrinkled held close—moving together with a grace and precision honed by time to a perfect rhythm.

Would that she could be a part of all of it — the courting and the marrying and the growing old together. *There's no chance, Mercy. When will you accept that fact and be content with your lot?* A tear escaped and she hurriedly wiped it away, all the while wishing she could erase the past as easily.

When she again searched out Norah and Daniel, she found her sister-in-law alone with the guests. Daniel wouldn't leave Norah without good reason. Esther! Was her little niece in trouble? Mercy half rose from her seat so that she might view the entire lawn. That was when she noticed the extremely tall man leaning against the front wheel of the Conestoga wagon loaded for tomorrow's departure. He and Daniel were

8

deep in conversation. From the look on her brother's face, Mercy concluded their topic was serious. Though she could hear nothing, she was unable to take her eyes from the stranger.

From years of habit, Mercy's left hand stole to the cap ruffle and, without conscious thought, she pressed it against her face. Although she couldn't see the newcomer's face, she played her game — trying to guess about a person from what she could observe. His shoulders and back were broad, and well-toned muscles rippled under his fringed buckskin clothing. He looked like an Indian, his ebony hair curling from around his fur cap and over the collar of his jacket. But then he turned slightly and she could see he had a full beard. No Indian, he. Powerful fingers gripped a long-barreled Kentucky rifle resting butt first on the ground and against his leg. *A woodsy from the west and Daniel's getting the latest information about the best route to take,* Mercy decided.

When they came to the back of the wagon, the stranger spoke up. "You chose well. These broad-rimmed wheels will keep you from bogging in the mud of the trails." His voice was deep and melodic. "You say you have two yoke of oxen?"

Daniel nodded, but Mercy couldn't hear his reply.

Daniel pointed in the direction of the barn, and the two men strolled from Mercy's view. Strangers were a commonplace occurrence at the Wheelers' place. Norah, from an affluent family near Richmond, loved to entertain, using the lovely things she had brought to the Shenandoah Valley with her. A successful farmer, Daniel had been able to provide for Norah a beautiful house with bedrooms enough for all the family, even Mercy, his maiden sister, and a spare one for the company who came often to the Wheeler house.

Mercy settled back on her bench. Looking again at the wagon with its white canvas roof, high and rounded with both ends open, designed to keep the

9

sun off and yet permit plenty of air circulation, she could still see the woodsy figure standing there.

Her thoughts wandered to the barn with the men. She closed her eyes and saw again the woodsman's long coordinated stride, watched him place his moccasined feet silently on the gravel path, and imagined a buckskin covered arm scratching the oxen between the ears. Somehow she knew he'd do that. She felt kindly toward him, even though she hadn't seen more than a rugged profile. His voice and manner of speaking, however, bespoke a cultivated refinement unexpected in a true woodsman. The man piqued her curiosity. Perhaps he would reveal something of himself to Daniel. She must remember to ask.

More guests arrived and Mercy's attention was drawn to them. She had no idea the farewell gathering would be so large, attracting people from all over the valley. Mercy smiled, knowing how pleased her sister-in-law must be.

"Say Daniel, where'd you hear of the land in Indiana?" called someone in a voice that carried over the group. People stopped talking to listen.

Daniel tucked his thumbs in his lapels and spoke with authority. "Congress recently purchased the central part of that far-off state in treaties with the Indians and then gave the land to Indiana. It's eighty acres of this 'New Purchase,' as it's called, that I intend to buy."

"What's the askin' price?"

"A dollar an acre, cash, for fine virgin farmland."

Mercy's attention, too, had been diverted from her musings and, when she glanced around again, the stranger was gone. Unaccountably she felt a peculiar sense of desertion. *Mercy, you silly goose!* she scolded herself. *You don't even know the man, will likely never even meet him. What's wrong with you?* But no amount of chiding removed the impression that something significant had transpired.

Her eyes wandered again to the big wagon which stood by the back door, packed full, and ready to travel in the morning. Mercy thought it strange-looking, with the front and back of the wagon built higher than the middle. Because of its shape, however, with the wheels removed, the wagon could be used as a boat.

Those wheels drew her eyes like a magnet—so large that Mercy would fit inside the spokes. Under the weight of a loaded wagon, they could crush anything in their path. The thought frightened her and she put the image from her mind.

Since so little was expected of her, her own needs were few, but still she mentally ticked off her belongings, carefully packed in one small trunk and stored inside. If she forgot anything essential, there would be little chance of remedying the oversight.

Looking fondly at Daniel, she couldn't help feeling he'd suddenly become afflicted with some mental flaw. Whatever had possessed him to pick up and move his family over hundreds of miles of unsettled land and through the dark woods of the Indiana country, she was still unable to imagine. Nor would Daniel elaborate beyond his declaration that life was getting too easy here in Virginia, and he wanted his children to have the experience of living life close to the elements, of discovering basic values. She only hoped he didn't come to his senses somewhere along the trail and wonder what they were all doing there.

Not that Mercy really minded the move. In fact, she sought seclusion and solitude as trusted friends, and had never learned to relax in Daniel's home, considering Norah's hospitable nature. Why, folks always felt welcome to drop in, unannounced. And now that the children were growing up, their friends, too, came and went at will. The house was always full of people, and Mercy was forced to spend more and more time shut away in her room, a fact that Daniel had decried earlier this spring.

11

The back yard slowly emptied as the guests, led by Norah and Daniel, made their way to the front. Mercy sighed deeply and leaned back to enjoy a few carefree moments. Her thoughts were interrupted, however, as a small girl in a blue print dress and a white linen cap came streaking around the corner of the house.

"Aunt Mercy, Aunt Mercy," shrilled the little voice.

Much as Mercy adored her six-year-old niece, Esther, right now she would have preferred to sit quietly, undetected, able to watch the party without the distress of participating. She didn't relish answering the same questions over and over as Norah was doing so patiently and graciously.

Spying her aunt, Esther dashed across the yard and came to a panting halt beside Mercy. "Why didn't you answer me?" she scolded. "I've called and called for you all through the house and the barn. The preacher's here and everyone's waiting for you so he can bless our trip."

"Oh dear, Esther. I quite forgot. Are you sure I can't hear him from this spot?"

Placing her arms akimbo, Esther shook her head. "Aunt Mercy, we're all 'posed to sit together as a family so all the folks can see us and cry over us."

Esther tugged at Mercy's hand, and laughing, she allowed Esther to drag her from her hideaway. Quickly pulling down the extra-long lace-trimmed ruffle of her lawn mobcap and holding it tightly against the left side of her face, Mercy permitted herself to be led across the lawn toward the neat, washed clapboard house and the benches set out on the front yard.

A tall masculine shadow crossed her path and swung into step beside her. Mercy's heart sprang into her throat and her hands grew suddenly cold. Having to deal with anyone other than the family always left her feeling flustered.

Watching his shadow on the ground before her, it

12

occurred to Mercy that this person might be the stranger she had seen conversing with Daniel earlier. She wanted very much to turn her head to look at him, but her neck seemed to have lost its ability to swivel.

A coarse voice drawled. "Howdy Ma'am. I bin huntin' you everywhere. You've sure succeeded in makin' yourself scarce."

This wasn't her buckskin-clad frontiersman. Fear leaped through her and flushed her face. *Oh, please, Lord—not another insensitive person wishing to satisfy his curiosity*. Mercy prayed and moved quickly forward.

Rough fingers curled around her arm, pulled her to an abrupt halt, and threatened to dislodge her grip on the cap.

"Are you always this rude to your guests?" he asked, his voice bitter and cold. "You bin hidin' since we wuz introduced this mornin'."

Panic bound her chest until she could scarcely breathe. "I don't recall having met you," Mercy managed to whisper, directing her remarks at his feet which blocked the pathway.

Why at every gathering must there be someone bent on tormenting me?

"Sure didn't make much of an impression on you, Miss Mercy."

Through a fear-induced haze crowding her brain, Mercy vaguely remembered an unkempt young man earlier attempting to engage her in conversation. Then she had excused herself and fled like a frightened quail into the house. Now there was no escape. Her tormentor was exceedingly strong, able if he chose, to snap the bones in the arm he grasped so tightly.

The rude man clutched her arm tighter and his voice hissed in her ear. "Well, I doubt you'll fergit me now."

A gasp escaped Mercy's lips.

"Mister, you let my Aunt Mercy alone!" Esther demanded. "You're scaring her!"

"Oh, I don't aim to hurt her none. Got me a little wager goin'. Bet the boys over there I could find out what's behind that mobcap."

An icy shiver ran through Mercy and she would have swooned had it not been for Esther.

"Aunt Mercy, look!" she cried.

Mercy's head turned in the direction of Esther's pointed finger. There, camouflaged by shrubbery fencing the yard, a number of gangling boys eagerly watched the proceedings. She flinched at their grinning mouths and brutish eyes, narrowed to slits. The sight of the mocking faces penetrated deep to join the ranks of countless others which nightly marched through her dreams.

Slowly the man resumed twisting Mercy's wrist. She must soon either let go of the cap or, with her fingers, pull it off.

"Please don't!" she begged. "Please leave me alone!"

"Shall I go for Father?" asked Esther, her eyes widening in fear.

"No need," said the stranger. "Jes' want to see what's so interestin' under that cap."

Mercy squeezed her eyes shut and felt tears wet her cheeks as she waited for him to jerk the ruffle from her face.

Suddenly the force of his grip lessened and then disappeared. When Mercy opened her eyes and looked about, the bushes were empty, and her persecutor, nowhere in sight.

"Wh—what happened?" she asked Esther.

"A giant came around the side of the house," replied the child.

"May the Lord heap blessing on him," Mercy breathed in gratitude as she cast about for her champion. "Where did he go?"

14

"I don't know. He just sort of disappeared." Esther reached for Mercy's hand. "We have to hurry, Aunt Mercy. Mama is going to be cross with us."

Straightening her cap and smoothing her dress as they walked, Mercy followed Esther down the path to the front yard.

Because of the encounter, they arrived at the meeting inexcusably late. Mercy felt every eye straining to follow their figures as they slid into their places on the front bench next to Norah and Daniel. Sitting on the other side of their father were Phelan, a squirmy ten-year-old, and Saba, twelve. On the end of the bench Mercy felt conspicuous, her face the target for all the curious. Daniel reached across Norah and squeezed Mercy's hand, his way of expressing his sympathy over the unavoidable ordeal. She thanked him with a wan smile.

Pressing the ruffle of her mobcap ever closer about the left half of her face and praying her heart and breathing rates would soon return to normal, Mercy attempted to ignore the stares, put her recent experience aside, and concentrate on the sermon. Since their planned journey was to take them into wild, unsettled country where there would be little chance for the practice of formal religion, this was likely to be the last such preaching she would hear for a long time. She wanted to store each precious word to examine in more peaceful moments.

Standing on a makeshift platform, the jolly-faced preacher opened his Bible. "My text today is taken from the one hundred and twenty-eighth Psalm . . . "Blessed is everyone that feareth the Lord; that walketh in his ways," the pastor began.

On the bench next to her, Esther wiggled. Being so fidgety was quite unlike the child. "What's the matter?" Mercy whispered.

"I don't know. My legs itch and it's getting worse and worse."

"Shush!" her mother cautioned.

A look of grim determination settled over Esther's face and the squirming stopped. Mercy again gave her attention to the sermon.

"For thou shalt eat the labour of thine hands: happy shalt thou be, and it shall be well with thee."

It seemed to Mercy that the preacher was making their trip sound too easy, when she knew better. Hadn't she heard the stories of Indians, killer bears, impenetrable earth that rejected a plow? The best news she'd received was that the large unsettled tracts of land were devoid of unthinking people and their cruelty. There she could go about her business without having to constantly clutch a concealing ruffle over her cheek. She could already feel the trees sheltering her, protecting her from the kind of incidents she must endure today.

What were those little pricks on her legs? She moved slightly. The tickly feelings persisted. She shuffled her feet.

"Aunt Mercy, you're wiggling," Esther whispered.

Here she was, a twenty-eight year old woman being justly chastised by a six-year-old child. But the trails of tickles continued to increase and grow more difficult to bear. Mercy looked at the stoic little Esther and wondered how she could sit so still if she were suffering the same irritation. The situation was rapidly growing worse, spreading up onto Mercy's thighs. Very soon she would not be able to sit with any degree of decorum.

She felt Esther give a violent shudder. Mercy looked down to see the child's hands clenched into little fists, knuckles white, gripping the skirt of her dress. Something was definitely crawling on them both. Slowly and carefully, in an attempt not to attract any more attention than necessary, Mercy examined the ground under the bench. Everything looked normal. She turned her head and inspected the leg of

16

the bench. Nothing. Then, looking down at the small log she and Esther were using as a foot rest, she barely stifled a scream at the sight of an army of ants. They marched in ranks across the log, up shoes, and disappearing under the dresses, continued along defenseless legs.

Taking no time for explanations, Mercy caught hold of Esther's hand and rushed her along the path down which they'd recently come and to the barn where it was safe to raise their skirts. Their limbs were covered with the little rust-brown creatures.

Mercy handed Esther an extra handkerchief, and working furiously, they swept the ants away.

"I don't know how you managed to sit still, Esther! You were so brave," Mercy said, giving her niece a big hug.

"I don't feel brave," she said in a weak thin voice. "I think I can still feel them crawling." Her chin trembled and china blue eyes filled with tears.

"I think I can, too." They both raised their skirts and inspected their legs once more. "I'm afraid we'll both have to believe there is nothing there but our imaginations." Mercy knelt before the white-faced little girl. "I think I can do it, if you can."

Esther gulped and wiped her nose. "I'll try."

Mercy folded her arms tightly around Esther. "I know you will," she whispered in Esther's ear. And then the little body began shaking as the sobs broke from her control. "Baby, baby, what's the matter?"

Now, Esther made no attempt to curb her tears, but clung to Mercy's shoulder, weeping out her misery. At last, she could talk.

"I pretended I wanted to go to the wilderness, but I don't. I want to stay here with my Boots and her new kittens." She pulled away and looked at Mercy with a tear-stained face. "You don't have to go. You could stay here and I'd stay with you."

"I'm afraid I have no more choice about going than

17

you do, Esther. We both must go and we must be brave about it, just as you were brave about the ants. It will be a great adventure and when we get to Indiana, I'll help you find a cat to replace Boots. That's a promise. Does that make you feel better?''

The little girl nodded and wiped her cheeks with the back of a pudgy fist.

Mercy pulled her cap ruffle firmly down over the side of her face. "Then, come." She took Esther's hand and brushed a kiss across it. "We must go back. Your mother will worry. We'll stop at the spring and you can rinse your face."

"Do we have to go up in front?" Esther asked as they walked along the well-used path.

"No. We'll find a place at the back. Then after the meeting, we'll explain to your mother and father what happened."

They arrived in time for the closing hymn "When Shall We Meet Again?" Mercy joined in reluctantly, feeling guilty. The truth was, she hoped she would never meet any of these people again. *In fact,*she thought, *I could live the rest of my life without neighbors to peek and pry. I would be perfectly happy without anyone but the family around. Could the constant fear of my face being seen be one of the reasons why Daniel decided to move to Indiana?*

Many of the people were in tears by the time the hymn was finished and the benediction pronounced. Norah and Daniel, with Saba and Phelan went up to stand with the preacher.

Mercy looked down fondly on her small companion. "Do you want to join your mother and father and say goodbye to the people?"

"Only if you'll come, too."

"No, I'd rather not, but I think you should."

"People will wonder why you aren't there."

"They won't miss me for a minute. Now run along."

Esther gave Mercy's hand a squeeze and ran happily to stand next to her mother.

The neighbors filed past, shaking hands and wishing the Wheelers well. Mercy gave silent thanks for the ants which had given her a legitimate reason to avoid the ordeal. After paying their respects, the guests drifted away to their conveyances and drove off to the schoolhouse where the dance was being held.

Mercy melted through the milling crowd and made her way into the house and the shelter of her room, away from the peering eyes—eyes that followed her into sleep at night and caused her to awaken, trembling from the recurring nightmare. Even though the story of Mercy's accident was known throughout the valley, she lived in constant fear that someone would come upon her in an unguarded moment to catch a glimpse of her disfigured face.

Though she little understood Daniel's sudden decision to move, she accepted it as an escape from bondage. Perhaps she would be released at last from the gripping terror and persecution she had endured for fourteen very long years.

CHAPTER 2

EARLY THE NEXT MORNING, the family drove slowly away from their home. Daniel carried the ox prod over his wide shoulders like a musket and marched at the front of the wagon as though he were setting off for war. Phelan cast the thin shadow of a boy not yet having begun his growth, but he stepped proudly by his father's side attempting to match him stride for stride as he helped drive the oxen. The women walked behind, Mercy consciously avoiding the tracks of the big wagon wheels, choosing instead to walk on the grassy side of the road.

They had gone only a short distance when Norah turned and looked back at the lovely rambling house, its freshly whitewashed walls sparkling in the bright sunlight. "I wonder if I'll ever have a house like that again," she said softly to no one in particular.

It still troubled Mercy that Daniel had so suddenly uprooted his family. It was clear from Norah's actions this morning that she wasn't looking forward to the next life in the deep woods. It appeared more and more that it was his decision alone, and this behavior was so unlike Daniel. He was normally thoughtful and practical, not given to hasty actions—certainly not those that were clearly unpopular with nearly everyone, particularly his wife. For her, until now, he had always shown the greatest consideration.

Mercy remembered well the night he'd broached the plan. Norah had paled at the idea, but said very little. Phelan thought it the greatest adventure that could possibly come his way. Saba, always quiet and unreadable, gave no hint of her feelings. On the other hand little Esther, never reticent about expressing herself on any subject, suggested that there were some good things and some bad things about moving; she'd have to think it over and decide which there were more of. They had all laughed at that bit of childhood philosophy and the discussion was ended. To Mercy's knowledge the matter had not been mentioned again.

Looking over at Saba, nearly as tall as her mother and solidly built like the Baldwin side of the family, Mercy watched her walk with firm steps in the track opposite Norah, staring straight ahead, expressionless. What she felt and thought right this minute, Mercy wondered. Not once in the time they'd been packing had Saba given a clue as to her feelings about the move. Mercy wished she were closer to Saba and could talk with her, but Saba lived in her own world and resented any intrusion.

Quite without warning, Saba turned into the same track and walked beside her mother. "Papa'll build you a fine house in Indiana, first off," she said, her voice possessing the strength and confidence of the young not yet exposed to the tragedies of life.

Norah gave her a wan smile and ran a limp hand across light blue eyes—eyes, framed by soft pale lashes, that had lost their fire and now appeared as shallow lusterless pools of misery. "Someday Saba, maybe someday." The escaping sigh rose audibly even above the rattling and crunching of the wagon.

Upon hearing her mother's distress, Esther stopped in the middle of the road and turned around. "I think I'll go back home. I don't want to be a pioneer," she said firmly. "I want my own bed and writing desk. I want Boots and my baby kittens." Little hands clenched and unclenched, and her chin jutted forward in an exclamation mark of stubborn determination.

"We've all had to make sacrifices," her mother said, impatience sharpening her voice. "You're no different."

Esther pointed to the sleek jersey cow tied behind the wagon. "Saba didn't have to give up her pet like I did."

"Only because we need Matilda to give us milk," Norah snapped.

Then, even this tiny flare of spirit vanished, snuffed out by sadness, leaving her listless and without strength to pursue the argument further. She gave a small shrug of her broad shoulders, tucked an errant wisp of golden-blond hair up under the white muslin mobcap, and plodded on after the retreating wagon.

Esther's feet seemed to take root. "Boots would keep the mice out of the barn," she said in defense of her pet.

Mercy put an arm around Esther's shoulders and turned her about. "We'll find you another cat as nice as Boots when we get to our new home. Boots would be terribly unhappy traveling with us. She might even jump out of the wagon and run away. Then her kittens would starve. This way you can always remember your pets still living useful lives there in their barn."

Her eyes rimmed with unshed tears, Esther finally permitted Mercy to guide her along. Together, they set their steps westward.

At first, though the road was smooth, other wagons filled with settlers crowded the dusty thoroughfare. At each meeting Mercy shriveled inside herself. But with the passing days, they encountered fewer and fewer travelers, and Mercy felt her nerves begin to unknot, and her spirits rose.

Then one evening just before dark, they arrived at a broad river, a black slow-moving shimmer in the fading light. On the opposite bank, lamplight already flickered weakly from a cabin window, and the wide flatbottomed ferry floated nearby in the water, anchored by a pole on shore.

Daniel stopped, and leaning on his ox prod, stared across the wide expanse. "No chance of the ferry coming over for us tonight," he said, disappointment shadowing his voice. "I've been told the boatman's recently taken a new wife and it's slowed his service considerably."

Mercy looked about at the large trampled area. The remnants of small campfires and piles of dung where animals had been tethered remained as mute evidence of others like themselves who had missed the last ferry and had been trapped on the wrong side of the river overnight.

Daniel turned from the water, his face lined with weariness but his voice firm. "Well, we can't stay here. The feed's all been eaten and there probably isn't a dry stick of wood within walking distance. Besides, it's too dangerous to camp near the river. A good chance we'd wake up with snakes for bed partners. If they were the wrong kind, we might not wake at all."

At this news a low weary moan escaped from Norah, and she grasped the spoke of a wagon wheel for support. Daniel rushed to her side and placed a protective arm around her. "I'm sorry, my dear. I shouldn't have distressed you with talk of snakes. Let me help you into the wagon. Your determination to walk all the way to Indiana is going to wear you out completely."

This time she didn't resist, and with Daniel's

assistance, clambered up over the huge wheel and onto the wooden seat. "Bring Esther to me," Norah instructed. "She's walked nearly the whole way, too."

Mercy picked up the tired little girl and carried her to her mother's waiting arms. Norah fussed over Esther, tucking a quilt around her and plumping a pillow for her to lie on.

Daniel turned the team and wagon around and they backtracked, lighting their way by a hooded coachman's lantern. At last they came to a meadow where the oxen and the cow could graze. While Daniel and Phelan unhitched the teams, Mercy milked Matilda, who complained loudly all the while at her treatment.

Esther stood, carefully eyeing the discontented cow. "I don't think Matilda likes being a pioneer, either."

"She'll like it when we come to where we're going. It's the getting there she doesn't like," Saba said as she scratched Matilda between the horn nubs.

Since it was dark and they were all too tired to hunt for firewood, their supper consisted of fresh warm milk and bread, the last of the food brought by their neighbors. Tomorrow they would begin cooking over an open fire.

Mercy and the children slept outside the wagon, giving Norah and Daniel as much privacy as possible. Saba and Esther slept together a short distance from the wagon, while Phelan, showing his independence, bedded down on the other side of the Conestoga. Mercy unrolled her bed not far from the girls and crawled between the quilts. She decided her bones must be getting used to sleeping in a bedroll spread on the ground.

By the time they arrived back at the river in the morning, several wagonloads of people were ahead of them, waiting in the chill of early morning. From habit, Mercy's hand flew to her cap. She pressed the white muslin ruffle against her cheek, even though her face was nearly hidden beneath the hood of her cape. Her nerves instantly tied themselves into familiar knots, and she shrank inside the cape, wishing she could become invisible.

From her sheltered spot behind Matilda, Mercy watched Norah's face, round and friendly, light at the sight of others like herself, traveling in the big white-topped wagons. Hurriedly, she climbed from the wagon and walked over to talk with the women grouped around a young girl holding a baby. Soon the Wheeler children joined a game of hide-and-seek already in progress, and Daniel entered into a lively discussion with the men.

Anguish filled Mercy. *Please, dear Lord, don't let these people be traveling in the same direction. I know that's selfish, but I don't believe I could endure such close company for such a long journey.*

Her prayer was interrupted by Daniel's arrival at her side. "Near as I can tell, it's going to be about noon before our turn comes to cross," he said gently.

"How can that be? We were first here, or rather last, yesterday."

"Apparently that doesn't count. Goes by who's first at the river come daybreak. Everyone else lines up behind."

"We should have bestirred ourselves earlier," Mercy said.

He put a firm muscular arm around her shoulders and gave her a hug. "We were all tired including the animals and needed the rest. We're making good time so this delay need not cause us worry."

Leaving her he returned to the circle of men. Everyone was in such good spirits that Mercy longed to join them. She had learned years ago, however, to keep to herself.

Shortly after the accident which had left its loathsome mark, an expectant mother had looked on Mercy's face and become hysterical at the sight. Her baby was later born with a severe birthmark on its face and she accused Mercy of being the cause.

After that incident, and in spite of the support of Norah's influential family, the feelings in the small farming community outside Richmond ran so high that the Wheeler family was forced to sell and move. Papa Wheeler thought it best to go as far as possible, so they didn't stop until they came to the northwestern frontier. No, Mercy sighed, it was better to leave well enough alone and remain, as usual, apart from the others.

Once across, the other travelers hurried on their separate ways and were soon nowhere in sight, a fact for which Mercy offered a silent prayer of thanksgiving.

As Daniel had predicted, ferrying such a large number of wagons had taken the morning, and the sun was nearly straight overhead when the boatman returned for the Wheelers.

"You folks ready to ship across?" the boatman called as he poled the ferry onto the bank.

"More than ready," Daniel answered as he and Phelan guided the oxen onto the boat. The stubborn creatures didn't take kindly to the rocking surface under their feet and required a stern talking-to before they would pull the wagon into a position which satisfied the ferryman.

At last, the loading accomplished, the boatman handed Daniel and Phelan each a pole and explained how they were to assist him in guiding the ferry in a reasonably straight line from this shore to the far one. The men positioned themselves on opposite sides of the ferry and dug their poles into the river bottom. Mercy, leaning against the sturdy railing, watched the small current-created waves slap against the upstream side of the boat as if attempting to punish it for obstructing their path.

"Hallo the boat!" came a distant shout, accompanied by the rapid clopping of hooves.

Brought on by anxiety over the arrival of strangers, the familiar unpleasant surge of weakness and nausea swept over Mercy, and she gripped the rudely built guard railing to steady herself. She withdrew inside the hood and pulled it closely about her face. Under the unrelenting rays of the noon sun, the dark gray cloak became oven-like, and she couldn't remember when she had been more uncomfortable.

"Is there going to be room for anyone else?" she heard Norah ask.

"Sounds like he's a loner with a couple a horses. Can always make room for a few more," the boatman assured her.

Never hurts to make as much money as possible on a crossing, either, Mercy thought. *Not to mention the manpower.*

"Thanks for waiting," she heard a strong masculine voice call over the scraping of the back bar as it was lowered. Two horses were loaded on, one of them appeared to be very large, judging from the heavy thudding sounds of its hooves. Both were blowing hard from the exertion of reaching the ferry.

There seemed something familiar about that voice. Mercy cast about, trying to place it.

Scraping sounds could be heard behind her. "Lady, would you move forward?" the rough voice of the boatman requested none too politely.

Mercy, her face nearly covered and her vision restricted, didn't know if he was speaking to her, and she had no intention of looking back to find out. She stood rigidly in the spot she had been assigned and prayed he would go away.

"Lady!" His voice, whip-like, slashed across her. "Move!"

Automatically clamping the hood against the side of her face, she jerked around to face him. A paunchy, sweatstained hulk towered over her. She took a quick step backward in an effort to escape. He waved toward the front of the ferry. "That way!" he growled.

With her throat suddenly gone dry, only a thin croak of fright escaped as she fled to the front of the boat. She fumbled for the railing and holding tightly, closed her eyes in an effort to quiet her stomach. At last her breathing steadied and she grew calm enough to open her eyes. Facing the far shore, she guessed the matronly woman standing there was the boatman's bride, awaiting his arrival. No doubt she had dinner prepared and had come to tell him. Mercy felt trapped and this caused her to withdraw even deeper into the protection of the cape.

"Hold on tight, Aunt Mercy," Esther cautioned.

The little voice startled Mercy, and she looked about to see Esther gripping the spoke of the front wagon wheel. The sight of the small child standing next to the heavy iron rim so weakened Mercy, that she barely had the strength to grip onto the railing for her own protection.

"Come stand by me. You can get a better hold here." To Mercy's amazement, her voice didn't betray the upheaval inside. She reached a hand to Esther and guided her to the front of the boat where there was a firm railing post to grip.

"You can take this pole and go to the front of the boat near the lady and the little girl," the boatman instructed the newcomer. "When I sound the word, everyone push hard as you can. Gonna take a bit of muscle to get this load off the bank."

Purposely keeping her back to the action, Mercy held tightly to Esther.

"Aren't you excited?" Esther asked.

"Oh my, yes," Mercy lied. "I've never ridden a ferry boat like this before. It's going to be a great adventure."

"Excuse me, ma'am." The voice very close behind her was gentle and deep.

She'd heard no footsteps. *He must be wearing moccasins*. Did that mean he was an Indian? She hardly thought so. He spoke with some hint of refinement and no accent. Mercy's heart raced in her chest like a captured bird beating against a cage. This was the woodsman who'd visited with Daniel at the farewell. What was he doing here?

"You're not standing in the safest place. You'd best stay away from the edge and next to the wagon."

Bowing her head into her cape, Mercy mumbled her thanks. Holding the hood tightly around her face, fearful that a capricious gust of wind might lift it, she took Esther's hand and went to stand next to the wagon box.

"We can see almost as well here, Aunt Mercy," Esther said.

"We surely can," Mercy answered quietly. Instead of looking out over the rolling river, however, her gaze locked on the huge wheel which turned ever so slightly as the ferry rocked against the fierce current.

"Push!" the boatman shouted.

Mercy could hear the grunts of the straining man as he leaned hard on his pole. The bank released its grip on the ferry with a loud sucking sound and it wobbled unevenly into the stream.

"You!" the ferryman's voice sounded, raspy and coarse. "We need your strength on this side now."

There was no reply to the request and Mercy, keeping her head covered, heard no sounds of walking. Curiosity overcame her fear. She pulled back the hood and turned her head just in time to catch a glimpse of a buckskin clad figure disappearing around the back of the wagon. She was sure it was the woodsman. What a coincidence that he should arrive at the ferry just as they were crossing. She hoped he would be leaving them as soon as the ferry touched the shore and he could get his horses off. This thought and the fact that he was on the other side of the ferry comforted her.

The breeze in mid-stream cooled the roasting effect of the cape and brought with it the delicate perfume of the flowers blooming along the banks upstream. The ferry rolled slightly under her feet and she found the motion rather pleasant. A soft rumble of the men's conversation told her they were fully occupied keeping the boat from drifting downstream, so Mercy relaxed a bit, confident she would be spared any surprise visitors.

When the ferry ground ashore, Mercy hastened to lose herself in the confusion of unloading. She hoped the goodbyes with the stranger would be short and they could travel on their way. However, as she watched from her hiding place in the rushes near the river, it quickly became clear her wish would not be granted.

Norah and the boatman's wife stood deep in conversation. Daniel, Phelan, and the boatman himself lounged against the wagon, visiting with the stranger as though they had all the time in the world. Saba entertained Esther in a game of hide-and-seek. It looked for all the world as though they were planning to settle right here.

Mercy crept from her secluded spot and sat on a large boulder shielded by lush bushes. In the excitement and emotion of leaving, Mercy had forgotten to ask Daniel about the man and, until now, he had not crossed her mind again. While she waited, she occupied herself as she had at the farewell party by examining the stranger's Indian-inspired clothing for some clue as to the man himself.

She had heard how hunters and trappers adopted this type of dress as the most practical for long periods in the wilderness. His garments, even the leggings and moccasins, were of soft leather. Just above the soles, the moccasins were ornamented with fancy beadwork, and his trouser legs appeared to be buttoned with silver fastenings. Sitting loosely atop his head was a beaver hat with two feathers cocked at a jaunty angle. Black shaggy hair curled across his forehead, then blended into a long untrimmed beard hiding his face almost as completely as her cape hid hers.

To Mercy, however, the man's size was the most notable feature. Since she took after the women in her mother's family, tiny boned and fragile, the frontiersman, who stood a head taller than the wagon wheel and dwarfed both Daniel and the boatman, seemed especially large. Even in the relaxed atmosphere, he stood erect, straight of back and flat of stomach.

If she listened carefully, she could pick out his unusually deep voice from those of the other men. Since no words could be distinguished, the tonal variations in the conversation were reminiscent of a soft chant, accompanied by the slapping waves and the soft whisper of the river.

She was struck by his serious demeanor. When the others laughed, he only smiled and when they smiled, his swarthy face, high cheekbones showing above the beard, remained immobile. There was more. Daniel and the boatman seemed tranquilized by the persuasive warmth of the noon sun, but the stranger remained ever alert, his eyes constantly darting toward the slightest sound, his body tuned like a fine instrument to respond instantly should the need arise.

After a few minutes, the women joined the men. A few words were exchanged, then Norah summoned Saba and Esther, and they all trooped over to the boatman's cabin. In a little while, Saba came carrying a plateful of stew to Mercy and sat down to visit while Mercy ate.

"We're to have company on our trip," Saba said. "Ben Tasker's going our way and he knows the woods. Says he isn't headed any place special, and Papa thinks it would be good to have another man along. Mama thinks it's a fine idea, too. Fact is, she's even smiling again.

Saba's news came as a blow to Mercy. The thought of having to evade yet another curious pair of eyes sent a nervous chill through her and made eating almost impossible. A deep sigh escaped. Even in the wilderness she wasn't to be free from hiding. *Dear Lord, what evil have I done that I should be punished so long?*

Then she felt ashamed. She had given up so little in comparison to Norah. How dare she sit here feeling sorry for herself. Things would work out. They had to!

CHAPTER 3

BEN TASKER STEPPED from the door of the boatman's cabin and blinked in the bright sunlight. To his surprise, the stew served for dinner hadn't tasted too bad, but the meat, tough and stringy, caught annoyingly in his teeth. He looked about for something to aid in removing it and in so doing, he discovered the woman sitting yonder near where the ferry had landed. *Strange little thing, hiding that way inside her cape. Must be powerful uncomfortable in today's heat.* Funny, he hadn't noticed her when he'd stopped by to talk with Daniel at the place in Shenandoah. Huddled on that rock tucked in the bushes, she looked like a tiny gray wren. Perhaps she was feeble-minded.

He located a slim reed to his liking and, squatting on his haunches beside the riverbank, cleaned his teeth and pondered. If she be not bright, that would make his task of getting the family safely to Indiana more of a challenge than he'd considered when accepting Daniel's offer. With time to think about it, he began wondering why he had agreed.

33

Been alone too much, Ben, my man. Getting lonesome and a mite touched in the head with no one to talk to. He still missed his family, particularly Genny and the little one, far more than he liked to acknowledge. Never found anyone who could come close to the wonder of Genny, but Esther tugged hard at his heart. Reminded him of his own little Sara near that age. Broke his vow, too. Swore he'd stay far away from any reminder of those family days, now gone and buried.

Well, the commitment was made to the Wheelers and, being an honorable man, he'd stick to it. A bargain was a bargain.

Having disposed of the last of his indecision, he turned his thinking to other matters. He straightened up and stretched. While the folks finished up inside, he needed to water his stock. Never taking his eyes from the woman, he strolled to the spot where the horses were tethered. As he approached, she turned so she faced the woods. Unusual. Most would be looking out at the water, folks being naturally drawn to the rhythm. Her actions reinforced his conclusion that she was weak in the head. Didn't seem likely she was dangerous, though. Norah wouldn't let her children close to someone who might hurt them. Even from the little he'd seen of Daniel's wife, he knew her to be the mothering kind.

He pretended to ignore the wee bird-like creature and busied himself with the horses. It looked like the family was going to be awhile, so he loosened the saddle on his big chestnut before he led them both down to water. After letting the animals drink their fill, he brought them up from the bank and back into the trees where he could tie them and let them graze a bit. He passed close to the woman and as he did, her hand flew to the hood of her cape, pressing it tightly against the left side of her face. Her movement, so rapid and practiced, startled him. *Maybe she's not slow-witted. Got some kind of affliction, though*, he mused as he finished with the horses. *Best I get on with finding out what it is for the safety of the others on the trip. Won't do for me to be preoccupied when I need to be alert.*

He set himself in her line of sight and deliberately walked toward her. She squirmed and her hand began to shake. Tiny though she was, she seemed to shrink even more, the closer he came. She looked so pitiful, huddled deep in that cape. Pangs of guilt stirred in him, knowing he was adding to her misery. He must meet her, though. It had to be done and maybe it was better like this, without the family to speak for her. They couldn't travel together and him not know what to expect. The fact that Daniel hadn't mentioned her added weight to his suspicions and justified his actions.

He stood in front of her and made a slight bow. "How do you do, ma'am. Name's Ben Tasker and I'll be traveling with you folks a spell." He watched her shoulders wilt and her whole body start to quiver. He wasn't quite sure how to proceed.

"Ma'am," he said in the softest voice at his command. "I mean you no harm. It's just that we're going to be together for quite a time and you can't go about hiding like this the whole way."

Still, she said nothing, but he could feel something akin to terror radiating from her. Maybe it was his size that frightened her. He sank slowly to the ground and sat Indian-style, his legs crossed in front of him. She spoke no word.

Well, he had nothing else to do right now. He could wait her out. Picking up a stick, he began to scratch in the dirt in front of him. And, because he failed to keep close guard over his thoughts, they strayed into forbidden territory—into the past he tried to keep locked away.

Genny. Wouldn't ever be anyone like Genny to

claim his affections. Genny—the only woman who'd ever come close to his size. Even with her robust girth and a laugh that often filled the village, she had understood his reserve, his need for solitude, and the craving to draw pictures that had elicited curious stares and even ridicule at times. She didn't seem to mind people laughing at her man hunched over squares of paper, drawing. She even encouraged him to teach what he knew at the little college nearby. How he missed her, even after all these years.

But he'd hated the laughter and the jeers, until at last, he put away making pictures, gave up teaching, and tended to farming. Still couldn't take a laugh at his expense. Froze him inside and turned him surly. Didn't have that problem anymore, though. Wild things didn't care how a man occupied his time, and he made sure no man saw him drawing.

Could it be only seven years since that fateful summer when the fever took his loved ones? It seemed much longer than that since he had begun roaming the frontier, counseling with the savages when he needed their advice and visiting the peddlers and settlement storekeepers when he needed supplies. Strange, how he'd run into Daniel, asking for advice about a wagon, and volunteered his opinion. After-wards, he wondered why he'd been so forward. Wasn't like him. Not at all.

Ben didn't know how long they sat like this, but she had to be near cooking inside that cape. This whole affair reminded him of Indians smoking out their prey by setting fire to a cabin and waiting for it to get too hot for the householders to remain inside. Indians had easy pickings when the hapless victims could stand it no longer and ran out. Ben continued to draw, but kept his attention focused on her. At last the shaking diminished and, as he had hoped, she was forced to abandon the cape.

She kept the left side of her face completely

covered, however, first with the hood of her cape and then, when it was removed, by clutching the over-sized ruffle of her mobcap against it. He stifled a gasp as he viewed the right side of her face for the first time. She was the most beautiful woman he'd ever seen! Glossy black hair, sweat-matted now, escaped from under the cap and lay against the nearly transparent porcelain skin of her forehead. There was no flaw visible in the fine texture of her skin. It was incredibly smooth with a satin sheen, and her nose, set straight, was delicately formed. The one eye he could see was blue. No, more like a blue-green — the color of the sea in the shallows. It was large and framed with long thick lashes that suddenly lay on her cheek like a smudge of soot as she shut her eyes against his astonished stare.

Before she closed them though, he'd read the message, the lost seeking look of a trapped animal wasn't reserved for those with four legs. *Poor little creature.* A tear escaped and rolled slowly over the high cheekbone and through the hollow below, reflecting the sunlight as it went. He found himself entranced by the sight. He'd never seen a woman cry like this, silent and motionless. When Genny had cried, which was seldom, tears gushed forth at a fearful rate and she bawled at the top of her mighty lungs.

The single tear arrived at the finely drawn square jaw, hung a moment, then dropped onto her white apron. Her full lips trembled and her chin quivered with the effort to restrain the tears.

However, from somewhere deep inside him sensations he thought long dead stirred ever so slightly. Had pity for this child-woman reduced to shambles his defenses, so carefully built against all emotions of the heart? It unnerved him to know that he sat before her as vulnerable as she. And yet he had no desire to escape her presence. He wondered if she realized this.

Probably not. She was too absorbed by her obsession with keeping half of her face covered to be aware of his feelings.

What lay behind that ruffle? A scar? A growth? A birthmark? It sickened his artist's heart to think of the nearly flawless countenance being marred. The disfigurement must be severe to cause such reactions. Or was she excessively vain and overreacting to a temporary blemish such as a boil? The more he considered this possibility, the less likely it seemed. Her actions were too well practiced and she gave forth no air of vanity.

At the sight of more tears following the first, he cleared his throat, "I'm sorry to have brought sadness. That was not my intent. I only wish to know you."

Silence greeted his overture of friendship. Since she kept her eyes closed, he felt free to continue his appraisal of her. He wondered what her skin would feel like. He'd touched satin once. Would it feel like that, slightly cool, grainless, glass-like? Long-buried sensations stirred once again and his breath caught.

Against all reason, he had to touch her, had to stroke that incredible skin, had to know if it felt as he imagined. Had to feel the bone structure under such a tiny, perfectly proportioned hand, like a normal-sized one scaled down to miniature. Had to show he meant no harm.

Gathering his courage and trying to imagine her reaction, he reached out and tentatively took the fragile hand lying so limp in her lap.

Her eyes flew open, and she opened her mouth as if to scream, but no sound came forth. She shrank from him and jerked the hand away. Idiot! This small gesture had been a grave mistake.

There was obviously nothing to do but wait on the lady. He still wasn't sure if she was of sound mind. Maybe waiting wouldn't be enough. Couldn't lose much in the trying, though, he decided, and so, letting his eyes drop, he returned to his idle sketching in the dirt.

He forced his thoughts away from her. He didn't like the poignant stirrings inside. Didn't want to feel anything but the cold numbness that had protected him these last years. Maybe he'd have to break his promise to the Wheelers, after all. Nothing was worth the risk of bringing the past to life again. Nothing!

A slight breeze whispered through the tops of the trees, and bird songs trilled in the air. Lower down, bees and insects created a lazy droning background to the shushing sounds of the river as it flowed through the reeds near the bank. A good river to fish, he thought. Too bad they weren't going to be close enough tonight to enjoy some of its fresh redeye. Then he squinted up at the sun. On second thought, at the rate these people were moving, they just might be.

His mind and emotions back under control, Ben dared to look at her again. She sure was a stubborn one. Still sat like a piece of Vermont granite, neither speaking nor moving. Probably had a lot of practice in waiting people out until they became so uncomfortable they left her alone. But he was stubborn, too, and he intended to out-wait her. He occupied the time by continuing to draw pictures of the animals he'd seen on his journeys, erasing each with a small branch from a nearby tree before creating another.

Finally, he felt her eyes on him. Maybe, if he kept his head down and didn't look at her, he could talk to her without frightening her speechless.

"What's your name?" he asked at last.

There was a long pause before she answered in a soft voice, barely above a whisper. "Mercy."

"Mercy," he repeated, rolling the word over his tongue to get the feel. It suited her. "I like it."

Again, there was a pause. "So do I."

The breeze picked up a bit and flirted with the hem

of her brown homespun dress, revealing heavy brown walking shoes. Her feet, crossed demurely at the delicate ankles, were so tiny and graceful they seemed more doll-like than real. He'd never seen a grown woman of this dimension before—only heard them described by others over a pint of ale in some inn.

At last she cleared her throat with a tiny cough. "What's your name?"

He could hardly believe it. She'd spoken without prompting. He wanted badly to raise his head as he answered, but he'd learned that this would probably drive her back into silence. "Ben Tasker." He was going to let her carry the conversation if she would.

Again silence descended between them, but he could feel the tension slowly draining from her. If the family would stay put a bit longer, he'd win her confidence.

"You draw very well," she offered at last.

"Never had any schooling in it. Just something I do."

"Do you draw on paper?"

"Not usually. It's not readily available in the woods, and that's where I spend most of my time."

"I have a few pieces of writing paper and some pens. Would you consider making a picture for me?"

"Now?"

"Oh no. When we have more time. I understand you're going to guide us so there should be some appropriate moments later on, don't you think?"

Her voice had risen to normal and she definitely was not feeble-minded as he had feared. He felt a great relief at the knowledge. It would have been a shame to waste that beautiful face.

At last, he answered her. "I'm sure there will be appropriate moments. However, I'm not sure I can confine my lines to paper any more. I'm used to having all the space I want."

"But you will try?"

He chuckled. Yes, she definitely was stubborn. He liked that. "Yes, I'll try," he promised.

Again, they sat in silence. He wondered if he dared look up at her. He sat considering if he should and what he'd say if he did. He couldn't just sit and stare at her, much as he'd like to. Ben had nearly made up his mind what to say when a loud shout rent the air, and Phelan burst from the cabin.

Ben raised his head and their gaze touched briefly. She smiled a shy smile that revealed small even teeth in exactly the proper proportion to the rest of her. Her face took on a soft glow and his heart gave an erratic surge. He returned her smile with a wide grin gone completely out of control.

He extended his work-roughened hand, and after hesitating, during which time he held his breath, she placed hers on his upturned palm where it seemed to be swallowed up there. He was almost afraid to close his fingers over the delicate fingers. But before she could have second thoughts, he stood in one graceful movement and helped her down from the rock. Then he picked up her cape from the rock and gathered it over his arm.

When he looked down at her, all he saw was the top of her head. He'd never been so conscious of his size before. She looked so like a very young girl, and yet she gave forth a woman's feelings, a woman's needs. Her nearness caused a constriction to grow around his chest that made breathing difficult.

He swore under his breath. He had to get away from her. She was arousing feelings he wanted forever buried—feelings for a woman, a home, a family. All the things he'd had once and had no more. The hurt from his loss still came near to strangling him some days. For that reason he promised himself, on Genny's grave, never to allow anyone to matter again.

He ran his thumb over the back of her hand. The tiny bone structure was perfect. He could feel no callouses to mar the softness. It felt as he had imagined it would—cool, silken, unmarred. Somehow, Ben forgot the vow, forgot to let go, and she made no effort to remove his hand. And so they walked toward the woods to fetch his horses.

CHAPTER 4

THIS WAS THE FIRST TIME in Mercy's adult life a man other than Daniel had held her hand because he wanted to. There were the infrequent times when she was helped from a buggy, but she couldn't recall now when that courtesy had last been extended her. Ben's hand felt warm and a bit rough, and there radiated from it a strength and sense of caring that penetrated her whole being.

She caught the look of amazement spreading over Daniel's face before she and Ben walked into the woods to bring back his horse and pack animal, and she chuckled silently her delight. Nothing would thrill Daniel more than for Mercy to find a loving man to take as a husband. He'd often said as much.

The trail was narrow and they were forced to walk very close together. Her pleasure at his nearness made her helpless to control the smile that broke over her face. Suddenly she had to laugh aloud. The laugh floated light and free out over the breeze, and she felt such a swelling in her breast, she could scarcely breathe. She wondered if he felt anything akin to her ecstasy. When she tried to look into his face, she found her head came only midway between his elbow and shoulder. She had to tip her head far back to see his eyes.

Ben stopped and looked down at her. "Pray, share with me your source of amusement. I haven't had a good laugh in years," he said, a smile playing at the corners of his mouth and his voice rich and sweet like thick dark molasses.

She looked up into deep brown eyes glowing with the sheen of fine silk—eyes that caressed her face gently in a way she'd never experienced. She understood now the reason for her laughter, but she hadn't the courage to tell him and so she said the first thing that crossed her mind.

"I only now pictured how we must look, you leading me along by the hand like a father would his errant daughter." There was a lilt, rippling and flowing through her voice, so that she didn't even recognize its sound. Her joy at his nearness and his gentleness was so great she couldn't contain it, and she laughed again.

Instantly, at the words and laughter, he dropped her hand as though scalded by its touch. His face changed to stone, his eyes narrowed slightly and turned opaque and dull. "Yes, no doubt it is an amusing sight." But there was no mirth in the tone.

The laughter died on Mercy's lips and her heart sank. In her naivete, she had unwittingly offended him and had no knowledge of how to repair the damage. Tears stung her eyes as she watched him leave her and walk on alone toward the horses. Standing, uncertain of the course she should take, she regarded him with a rising ache in her heart. The first person in years, other than family, to show her any compassion, and she had alienated him in an inept and thoughtless fashion. Perhaps if she waited, he would return this way. Meanwhile, she tried to think of something to heal the breach.

However, he took a great deal of time attending to the pack horse, carefully checking each hoof and then rearranging the packs as though they weren't properly balanced. At last, she realized he wasn't coming back and with this recognition came a shuddering sigh. The habitual sag returned to her shoulders and, bowing her head, she hurried toward the river to join her family who were nearly ready to begin the journey again.

How dare she think she might have a normal and happy experience with a man, however brief. No man would ever want her. Years ago, a few young men had come to call, but when they'd seen the scar, they hadn't come around again. Ben Tasker had pierced her guard with his determined waiting, but no more. She hardened her heart and vowed she would not ever again trust any man. She hurt enough inside without deliberately seeking to add to it.

As she neared, Daniel looked up from harnessing the oxen. "That was quite a sight, the two of you walking hand in hand."

"Yes, I'm sure it must have been. I'm not surprised you found it amusing." The cold that ran through her, however, chilled her bones as though deep winter had suddenly replaced the spring day. Her hand that had, a few minutes earlier, nestled warm and snug in Ben's gentle grasp now hung at her side, icy and stiff in its lonely coldness.

"You folks ready?" Ben's voice boomed from up the road.

She didn't glance in his direction, but rather pretended her attention was needed elsewhere. When, at last, she could avoid it no longer, she began slowly walking up the road behind the creaking wagon. Ben stood with his animals across the tracks as though to block any progress along the roadway. It was obvious even from a distance that he had no intention of coming back to join them, but would wait where he was until they met.

45

Then she saw it—her cape draped carelessly over his saddle. She'd forgotten he was carrying it. She knew he didn't want to talk with her again and yet, what was he to do with the cape?

Straightening her shoulders against the encounter, she quickened her step and passed the slow-moving wagon. When she arrived where Ben waited, she reached up and wordlessly retrieved the cape. Her vows of a few moments earlier were forgotten in his presence, and she desperately wanted to explain, to tell him of the joy he'd brought her. But everything that raced through her mind sounded inane, and worse, completely inadequate to justify her laughter.

She couldn't tell him that it wasn't the picture they made together that had caused the laugh, but the rush of pure joy that touching him and being with him caused. Couldn't say she didn't care how they looked together, had only thought of it in the moment when he'd asked why she laughed. Their having been together was the important thing to her. He made her feel things she never had felt before and the warm spark he lit dispelled briefly the cold darkness that continually dwelt within. Though it lasted only a short time, the spark burned long enough to let her know such a glow existed. Those few moments exposed a completely unexplored world of emotions to her. Loving feelings, like clear bubbling springs, had risen from her heart and overflowed, filling her until she could no longer contain the gladness. She had to laugh. But how could she tell him when she wasn't sure she completely understood it herself? Wasn't sure he'd even care to know.

She stood, head bowed, and gripped the cape, trying to fight through the soundless space separating her from Ben. Prayed for some word to erase the mountain she had created between them and over which she seemed helpless to climb. She could feel his eyes on her, and she begged God for the courage to lift her face to meet his. Then, she heard the saddle creak as he settled his weight in it. Her head snapped up, but she was too late. All she saw was his figure retreating down the road.

Instinctively, she raised her arm toward him. Opening her mouth to hail him back, the words stuck in her throat, and no sound broke the silence but the clip clop of the horses' hooves as they moved steadily up the road away from her. Ben sat ramrod straight in the saddle, his back and neck rigid. The saving moment had passed.

Behind, she became aware of the grinding crunch of the wagon wheels over the rocks, warning that she'd best move or be ground under. She flung the cape over her shoulder and stepped out in a brisk walk ahead of the wagon.

The road they took on this side of the river was much less well-traveled. It wasn't nearly so wide nor smooth and it required constant attention to avoid rocks, tree roots, and holes with standing water. With each day's travel the tracks became more narrow and rough until the Wheelers reached the great woods where there were no roads at all. Here they traveled on muddy paths winding among the giant trees. Ben Tasker located the best route for the wagon and guided the family by chopping blazes on the trees for them to follow.

The woods were full of game—rabbit, squirrels, and many small rodents. Daniel stopped the wagon often so they could watch a deer feeding or see a fox, wolf, or panther slink past. Daily, from this rich supply, Ben provided fresh meat which he left lying along the path for them to find. But they rarely saw him.

As the days drew on, the travel began to take all the energy Mercy could summon. The nights didn't seem quite adequate to erase the exhaustion of the day, and she never felt fully rested when she awoke. Norah complained continually that the old thick-trunked trees stood so close together they made her feel like a prisoner. Walking became such a chore, she rode with Esther in the wagon much of the time. Phelan helped his father guide the oxen. Saba, never one with whom Mercy could share confidences, grew even more remote and walked ahead of the wagon much of each day, seeming more and more to prefer her own company.

Since they so rarely met anyone traveling and since Ben scarcely ever came near them, Mercy began to feel less threatened and no longer bothered to cover her face. The family had long ago grown used to her disfigurement. The children had never seen her without the ridged discolored scar that ran from her hairline across her cheek and ended abruptly at the jawline. She had offered to keep it bandaged to lessen the offensiveness to the eye, but Daniel wouldn't hear of it. Since one half of her face was unblemished and beautiful, he said he didn't want it marred in an attempt to cover the other.

Poor Daniel. He still suffered such guilt over the accident. She wished there were some way she could relieve his self-condemnation. She knew if she wasn't around constantly to remind him, the pangs would grow less sharp. However, he wouldn't agree to her leaving. In truth, since their parents had died, she had had no other choice, except perhaps to have a small cabin built somewhere in the woods. Although she dreaded meeting people, she realized the alternative of living with Daniel and his family was far safer for a woman alone, and so she stayed. By so doing, here she was, traveling into deeper woods than she had ever imagined.

Because the sun couldn't penetrate the tangled treetops, it was always damp and shady in the forest and Mercy found it more and more difficult to remain cheerful. She enjoyed the warmth of the sun, and each day the longing to feel it on her back and arms grew greater. She hoped their land in Indiana wouldn't be completely shadowed. That would be hard to endure, and Norah would become even more unhappy.

Mercy entertained herself by watching the many different kinds of birds that flew overhead. There were flocks of pigeons so large that when they settled for the night, the branches of the trees would crack and break under the load. Her favorites were the brightly colored little parakeets darting about crying "skeet, skeet, skeet." She considered catching one and putting it in a cage. Then, thinking about her own imprisonment and how unhappy it made her, she couldn't bring herself to inflict the same kind of misery on any other living creature.

One day, Mercy looked up to see Ben riding through the trees toward them. She quickly dived behind some bushes while Daniel hastened to meet him. The two men walked away, deep in conversation. Mercy could make nothing of their talk except through their motions. They kept pointing into the forest, but even by straining her eyes, she was unable to see anything more than trees, dense, constructing, overwhelming.

Returning to the family waiting around the wagon, Daniel said, "Ben's tracked the country for miles on both sides of our position. It's steep down to the river, but he's blazed the best trail he could find. He thinks if we camp here tonight, rest the oxen well, and start fresh in the morning, we should have no problem."

"I think we're ready for some rest," Norah said. "Come children, gather the wood, and we'll get a fire started." Turning to Daniel, she asked, "Is Ben going to join us this evening?"

"I've invited him. He's gone to find some meat for our supper. When he returns, perhaps you can add to my invitation."

"He makes himself so scarce, I haven't had the opportunity to thank him for providing our daily food. It would be nice to visit with him and share the bounty he supplies."

Mercy busied herself, gathering small dry sticks and grass for the fire. *How like Norah*, Mercy thought. *Even here in the dark woods, she's planning a dinner party.* Mercy piled her contribution on the growing mound and gathered Esther to her while Daniel produced the tinderbox and lit the fire.

"Is there something I might do to help?" Mercy offered.

Norah looked up from peeling the potatoes. "Yes, keep Esther at a distance from the fire."

Little Esther had become Mercy's primary assignment as they traveled. When Norah and Daniel were married, Norah had made it a firm rule — the kitchen and its duties were hers. "Saying is, 'there's no house big enough for two women,' but I think it's the kitchen that's too small," she'd said. Mercy was encouraged to help with the children when they came, and to clean, but she never did more in the kitchen than menial tasks such as shelling peas or snapping beans. How she longed to prepare a full meal.

"Come, Esther. While it's still light, let's find a stick and you can practice writing your letters in the dirt." Mercy found a spot a distance from the camp where the ground was packed and bare as if a deer had bedded there. With a bit of tidying, the ground was soon free of dead grass and leaves and Esther carefully scratched her first letter. "A," she intoned. "B . . . C . . . "

As Mercy sat on a log, watching and guiding Esther, she became aware of eyes staring at her back. Not knowing if they were animal or human, she quickly covered her face, then cautiously inched her way around until she could look behind. She saw nothing and yet the feeling persisted. *Indians!* The thought made her scalp crawl.

Unaware of the possible danger, Esther continued to drone out each letter as she produced it, and Mercy automatically nodded her approval with each successful completion.

"Aunt Mercy, you're not paying attention to me," Esther complained.

Daniel had drummed at the children to mind without question, but Mercy felt they deserved some explanation. "True, I'm not giving you my full attention. I think there may be an animal watching us from the woods. Please go on as you were so as not to cause alarm. I shall continue to watch," she said in a quiet calm voice.

Esther, apparently detecting no fear in Mercy, returned to her letters, while Mercy let her gaze play over the forest. She was rewarded at last by a flash of fawn-colored buckskin. It happened so quickly, she couldn't be sure whether it was a man or a deer. She wished she knew which, for Daniel must be alerted to real danger.

"I've done all my letters three times with no mistakes. Can't I do something else now?"

Mercy smiled, "If you can do them that well, then it's time to do some ciphering. Do two plus two for me." Mercy's father had insisted all his children learn the rudiments of reading, writing, and arithmetic. Thank heaven, Daniel had exacted the same requirement of his children. Phelan and Esther were eager students, and Phelan could already read the Bible and cipher as well as Daniel. Like her mother, Saba disliked the learning and grudgingly sat for her time.

There it was again! The movement was soundless, but the distinctive fawn color showed briefly, now dangerously close to camp. This time she glimpsed black hair. It could very well be Ben, but if it were not and they were set upon by Indians. . . .

When Ben at last stepped into the small clearing, carrying two rabbits already skinned and ready for the

51

pot Norah had steaming over the fire, Mercy breathed a sigh of relief. What a start he had given her!

But why had he stared so long and hard at her? Had he seen the scar? She prayed not.

She and Esther continued ciphering until Norah called them for supper. Esther joined the family, but Mercy stayed where she was, being careful to turn her right side to the camp. Saba brought her a plate of stew and a cup of fresh milk. Bless Matilda. Even with the long days of walking, she still produced a full bucket of milk each morning and evening.

While Mercy wasn't close enough to join in the conversation, she could hear what was being said.

"Going to be a hard day tomorrow," Ben said. "That hill will be difficult to negotiate, but I've found a good spot to camp on the other side of the river."

"Will the oxen have the strength to ford the river after the work of getting down?" Daniel asked.

"River's not very wide or deep and it has a good gravel bottom. There's no place to camp on this side. You'll have to make it to the other side." Ben didn't look up from his plate as he spoke.

"Is there anything I should do to prepare the inside of the wagon?" Norah asked.

"Just make sure everything's tied down tight. We should have no problem with the teams well rested. You've good strong animals and they're trained." Ben handed his empty plate to Norah. "Mighty fine stew, ma'am. Appreciate your inviting me to share it."

"It's surely the least we could do when you have provided for our needs so generously." Norah smiled at his praise.

Ben stood and leaned against the huge rear wheel. It was dark now, and the firelight danced through the spokes, making them shimmer as though they were moving rapidly. Mercy stared until she felt herself being drawn into the hub and united with the wheel as it sped along. Suddenly she wanted to scream and only prevented it by clasping her hand over her mouth. Daniel always said her imagination was far too active for anybody's good.

She collected herself and carried her plate to where Saba was washing the dishes. While Mercy carefully avoided looking at Ben or the wagon wheel as she walked past, she felt his eyes follow her, and the image of the turning wheel continued, vivid.

CHAPTER 5

MERCY AWOKE FROM TROUBLED DREAMS she vaguely remembered. A strong bitter taste filled her mouth and gray weariness wrapped itself about her like a shroud, both serving as reminders of the night.

With eyes still closed as a last defense against the newly arrived day, she lay in her bedroll listening to the early morning sounds. The sleepy chirp of birds nesting high in the trees above her announced the rising of the sun, a sight the Wheeler family had been denied for days. How she would praise the Lord when she could again behold that miracle, taken for granted until this journey.

Wood gathered last night snapped and crackled as Daniel broke the dry branches into shorter lengths. The pieces thudded together as he tossed them onto the teepee shaped pile she envisioned him building in the fire pit. Then, silence. She imagined him, trousers pulled carelessly over his nightshirt, and hair standing at odds with his head, shuffling to the wagon for the pot in which hot coals were kept in case the fire burned out in the night. The clank of the lid as he removed it told her she was right. She listened for the soft rush accompanied by tiny poppings to tell her the fire had caught. Then, water sloshed in the big iron pot as Daniel filled it and set it to heat over the crackling fire.

"Everybody! It's morning and time to wake up," Esther's cheery voice rang through the woods. When she awoke, she thought it time for everyone else to be about also. Since turning two, Esther had taken upon herself the task of rousing the unwilling from their beds, and her tenacity in fulfilling this self-assigned duty had remained undiminished through the years. "Phelan!" she shouted. "Are you up?"

"Up and dressed, you sleepyhead."

"Saba?"

A soft laugh bubbled into the fresh morning air. "Esther, I'm in the same bed as you. You know I'm awake."

Esther giggled at her little joke. "Papa?"

"Here, Esther."

"Where?"

"By the fire, putting the logs on."

Esther continued roll call at the top of her voice. "Mama?"

From inside the wagon came the muffled reply. "Good morning, Esther. I'm up and getting dressed."

"Ben?" Silence greeted Esther's query. "Ben?" she shouted again.

"I think he's already up and gone to scout our trail this morning," Daniel said.

Esther always saved Mercy until last because Mercy still played little games with her. "Aunt Mercy?"

Mercy pretended to be sleeping soundly.

"Aunt Mercy, you have to get up," Esther commanded.

Mercy could hear the rustle of bedclothes being turned back and pictured Esther struggling into her shoes. Then, little feet pounded over the deep duff of the forest floor as she came flying to coax Mercy awake. This had become ritual through the years, and today Mercy was especially glad for the precious little girl. Hopefully, she could chase away the dark dream-shadows which still hovered over her mind.

While Norah and Daniel finished packing the wagon and Saba entertained Esther with finger games, Mercy took a walk, following the blazes Ben had cut in the trees. She wanted to see for herself what they faced this morning. It took only a few minutes until she was standing on the edge of a moderately steep slope, overlooking a valley. Here, the trees grew much less dense and tall. From the blackened trunks of snags left standing, it became obvious that a fire many years ago had blazed through this part of the forest and cleared a wide swath along the side of the hill. Mercy's heart leaped at the unexpected open sky and she threw her head back and drank in the blue-cloud-puffed space. The sun was at her back, but she could see it light the treetops of the valley and in the distance, turn the river into a glistening silvered ribbon.

Thank you God, for a beautiful day and for granting my plea to see the sun. She stood drawing strength from the sight and praising God in her heart for giving her the eyes with which to take delight in His handiwork. Mercy stood, absorbing the expansive view and giving thanks until, at length, her meditation was interrupted by Esther's call to breakfast.

"Coming, Esther," Mercy answered. Gathering her skirts to protect them from the snagging underbrush, she picked her way back to the wagon, dwarfed by the huge trees.

Breakfast was a simple meal, cornpone cooked in the iron spider and spread with strawberry jam given as a parting gift to the family. Together with fresh milk from the faithful Matilda, it was a satisfying repast.

56

When she finished, Mercy cleaned her plate and hurried to roll up her bed, ready to pack in the wagon. As she completed her task, she heard Ben's low rumbling voice and metal struck metal, signaling that Norah was preparing him something to eat. Mercy finished tying the blankets together and, taking a circuitous route back to the wagon to avoid being seen, she stored her bed.

Having completed the only task allowed her, Mercy stood, wondering what to do. Perhaps she could vanish and meet the wagon at the crest of the hill. But she did want a peek at Ben before she left. She loved watching the way he moved, cat-like in his grace. The muscles of his legs rippled visibly under his tight-fitting leather trousers, much as did those of the panther under its skin. She had watched Ben walk over ground littered with dead leaves and small sticks and never make a sound. He didn't appear to concentrate on placing his feet, but like the wild animals, seemed to sense instinctively where to step.

"Mercy," Daniel called. "If you can hear me, please come. Ben needs to talk with all of us."

Pulling her cap from her pocket, she hastily pulled it over her hair and pressed the ruffle against her face. When she arrived at the campfire, everyone was already gathered around, and she slipped behind Norah's stout figure where she could hear but not be readily seen.

Daniel nodded to Ben. He scanned the group, looking carefully at each one until he came to Norah. His gaze rested firmly on her, but he let his eyes slide past Mercy to Saba. "I asked Daniel to let me talk with you. By taking the path we have, there's no other route across the river without going days out of our way. If we're to get the wagon to the bottom in one piece, it's going to take the help of everyone here."

Mercy could feel the tension building inside and her palms turning slick with perspiration. The hill hadn't looked that steep to her, but with a wagon it must be a different matter.

Ben continued. "Daniel will tend the oxen. I'm going to tie some ropes along the uphill side of the wagon. The more weight we can get pulling against the slope, the greater our chances are of successfully making it down. I want all of you, except Esther, to join me in pulling on those ropes. Dig out gloves to protect your hands against rope burns and give you a firmer grip."

"That's not fair," a small voice said. All eyes turned to regard Esther, her little chin crumpling into the tremble that signified the beginning of tears. "Why can't I help? I know I'm not big, but I would pull very hard."

Ben knelt before her. "I know you would, but I have another task for you that's equally important. Someone has to take care of Matilda and lead her down the hill. Do you think you could do that?"

At the suggestion, Esther swelled with importance and a smile brightened her face. She nodded vigorously.

"I thought you could," Ben said and reached to gently adjust the cap sitting askew on her head.

Mercy watched his tender gesture and the memory of the few moments when he had held her hand flooded over her.

Ben rose slowly to his feet and, without a backward glance, moved to adjust the saddle on his horse. "I'll ride ahead and meet you at the spot where we start down."

His voice was rough with emotion and Mercy wondered at the change. Was it Esther who had affected him so? Ben Tasker was a strange and complex man. Why was she drawn to him, when it became clearer with each passing day that he would never again pay her more than the barest attention.

Esther dashed to Mercy, grabbed her hand, and

began pulling. "Come on, Aunt Mercy, help me unfasten Matilda."

Mercy, grateful for an excuse to leave the group, allowed herself to be led away. "Ben has given you an important responsibility. He must think a great deal of you."

"He does," Esther said in all innocence. "He tells me stories when he's in camp, and he even takes me for rides on Constant."

With deft fingers Mercy untied the cow and handed the rope to Esther. "Who's Constant?"

"His riding horse," Esther said, leading Matilda away from the wagon and holding her rope so she could nibble the buds from nearby bushes.

Mercy followed and stood near Esther, continuing their conversation. "What a strange name."

"That's what I said. Ben said he bought her at a time when the horse was the only constant thing in his life." Esther looked up at Mercy. "I don't understand what he meant."

Mercy's heart wrenched. "I don't, either," she said softly. "I don't, either."

Further contemplation of Esther's words was postponed as Daniel cried, "Let's move out!"

With a creaking and groaning that overshadowed all other sounds in the forest, the wagon moved reluctantly from its spot. Esther and Mercy fell in behind. Esther continued to chatter, but Mercy paid her words scant heed. What had Ben meant, *the only constant thing in his life*?

When she and Esther arrived at the meeting spot, Ben and Daniel were already busy tying ropes into the big iron rings bolted along the sides of the wagon.

Ben pulled back, testing each rope after he fastened it. "These aren't as long as I'd like, but they'll have to do," he said. "I'll haul on the first rope. Norah, you take the one over the front wagon wheel. Phelan, stand next to your mother."

They both slipped on gloves and grasped the ropes Ben indicated.

"Saba, you hold the rope next to Phelan."

Mercy's heart vaulted into her throat. He was going to have to speak to her. She'd wondered if he would acknowledge her presence at all. He bent down and picked up the rope from the ground. He didn't hand it to her immediately, however. Rather, he carefully made several knots along its length.

Curiosity overcame her reluctance to speak, and fixing her courage, she asked, "Why are you doing that?"

"So you'll have handholds. If your hand begins to slip, you can let go and grab lower down on the rope."

She could discern nothing in his voice to indicate that he regarded her as different from the rest of the family. Then, for the first time since their disastrous encounter by the river, he looked at her. His eyes were opaque pools which reflected their surroundings but divulged nothing below the surface.

"You can't possibly be of any help if you're using one hand to clutch your cap to your face. It's going to take both hands." His voice, steady and low, gave no hint of emotion. He might be speaking to Matilda instead of Mercy.

At his words, Mercy's face grew hot with embarrassment and she ceased being nervous over Ben's presence. He had just posed a much larger problem. Frantically, she began casting about in her mind for a solution. She hadn't revealed that scar to any but family for years, and she didn't intend to make today the exception if she could help it.

Norah dropped the rope and removed her gloves. "Come, Mercy. I have an idea."

Gratefully, Mercy followed her to the back of the wagon.

From a small case of fabric scraps, Norah selected

a piece of pink georgette. "We'll pull the cap ruffle over your face and tie this around your head to secure it." As she spoke Norah proceeded to execute her plan. "There now. It hides everything beautifully."

Her eyes brimming with tears, Mercy gave a tremulous smile of thanks.

"Should have thought of that years ago. We can make you more scarves, and you won't have to go about one-handed when strangers come."

"Are you ladies ready?" Daniel called.

"Ready," Norah answered, shutting the case and returning it to its storage place.

Mercy took a deep breath and walked to her position. The rope, fastened in the ring directly above the back wagon wheel, lay like a long venomous snake coiled to strike. She did wish she could share in the excitement this break in the daily monotony stirred through the rest of the family, but her feelings of apprehension crowded out any sense of exhilaration.

Reluctantly she picked up the distasteful rope. She tested the feel of it. Ben was right. The gloves and the knots did help.

Ben took his station in front. "All ready, Daniel."

Daniel cracked the whip in the air and the oxen strained to move the wagon sunk deep in duff undisturbed for centuries. Mercy watched the huge rear wheel begin to turn, little by little, until it was revolving at its usual rate. The wagon dipped over the crest and began its diagonal descent across the face of the hill toward the river and the valley beyond.

Mercy walked alongside, keeping her rope from tangling in the underbrush. At least, there were no big trees here to impede their progress. "How are you coming with Matilda?" she called to Esther.

"Just fine. She's too busy eating to notice much. When she raises her head to chew, I pull her along some more."

Although the wagon picked up a bit of speed, Daniel kept the oxen under control. Mercy saw some large boulders protruding in their path immediately ahead, and Daniel guided the wagon a bit steeper down the hill to avoid them. They all flipped their ropes over the rocks, except Mercy. She didn't cast hers high enough and it snagged on the jagged points on top. At the same time, the wagon began slipping sideways.

"Haul!" Ben shouted.

The family all laid back on their ropes, but Mercy's rope was behind the wagon. As she ran to get in position, she tripped on a piece of the rock outcropping. She managed to hold on to the rope but lost her balance. The wagon lurched forward and sideways, pulled her off her feet, and slammed her into the back wheel. Before she could right herself, her skirt became caught in the axle and it began to wind her up against the side of the wheel. With each turn of the wheel, she could feel herself being drawn closer and closer toward the spokes and the wide heavy rim. The cloth bound itself tighter and tighter about her legs. Frantically, she jerked at the fabric with her one free hand. It was a useless gesture for, in her effort to stay back from the menacing rim, she pulled away rather than leaning forward to create some slack. The folds in the material cut into her skin like whips curling about tender calves.

Her heart, already pounding dangerously, began racing. *I'm surely going to die*, her mind beat in rhythm with her heart. *I don't want to die, Lord. Please, I don't want to die now—this way*. These thoughts caused her heart to beat even more wildly. She grew lightheaded and her hands and feet began to tingle. If she had not been so tightly wrapped, she would have surely fainted.

The rest of the family, concentrating on keeping the wagon from overturning and rolling to its destruction down the hill, did not notice her plight, and she was too frightened to scream.

Please, Lord—help me ! Mercy's rational mind was fast numbing with the terror. Her legs were nearly bound together as her dress twisted tighter and tighter around the axle. As the last slack in the full garment disappeared, Mercy dropped the rope. She almost stumbled again, but managed to right herself and grab hold of the spokes, one in each hand. Placing her feet on the rim of the wheel between two spokes, she now rode inside the wheel, raked against it like a felon straddled for a beating.

As she rose in the air she could feel the tension on her skirt loose slightly, for now she rotated with the bouncing wheel. The hub turned hard against her midsection and restricted her breathing. With the next revolution her head approached the ground. What if she wasn't far enough in the wheel and her head didn't clear? She'd be knocked senseless, fall off, and be run into the ground, just like her nightmare. Clouds of choking dust rose from the rolling sliding wheel, burning her eyes and sending her into paroxysms of coughing.

Now she hung upside down. Miraculously, she felt no searing pain, no pummeling blows of rocky ground against soft flesh. She started to fade in and out of consciousness, aware of little more than that the wheel had moved on around and she was in a standing position. She wanted to cry out, to release the abject fear sealing her throat. She felt a scream rise from deep within but the tensed muscles of her throat built a dam, making it impossible to call for help.

Even though she was nearly unconscious, self-preservation took over, and she clutched the spokes in a death grip. After the first rotation, she closed her eyes against the revolving world. Dazed with shock, she rode silently through several dark eternities.

"Oh, my God!" Ben bellowed. "Daniel, stop! Stop the wagon!"

The wheel made several more revolutions before they were able to halt the heavy load. Then she felt eager hands tugging and pulling, trying to untangle her dress.

"She's standing on her head! She can't stay that way!" Daniel shouted, alarm causing his voice to crack like an adolescent.

"Her dress is wrapped so tight, I can't find enough slack to unwind it!" Norah sobbed, her frustration reducing her efforts at freeing Mercy to random pluckings.

Mercy was only dimly aware of the futile struggle. Hysteria created an unreal world in which she must surely die, and she sank without objection into a floating void.

"We're going to have to take it off, then," Ben's bass voice rolled over the frightened group. "Get a blanket, Norah. Saba, crawl under the wagon to the inside of the wheel. Unlace her corset. Phelan, tend the oxen. Esther, find some grass for Matilda, but stay close by."

Mercy could feel Saba's strong young fingers yanking at the corset strings. Strong hands grasped her shoulders and held her, relieving the pressure from her exhausted arms. The waistband went slack.

"The skirt's wound so tight in the axle, I can't get it any looser," Saba said, her voice quavering under the strain of her task.

"Then we have no alternative but to cut her out of her skirts," Ben said. "Norah?"

"I have scissors right here. Daniel, you spread the blanket so we can wrap her up as soon as she's free."

Mercy could hear the snip of the scissors as Norah cut away the confining garments. Large firm hands encircled her waist. The instant she was free and she felt her body start to fall away from the wheel, those hands, Ben's hands, lifted her and gently laid her on the sun-warmed blanket. He wrapped her inside the warmth and picking her up, cradled her in his arms.

Now that she was safe, she began to shiver violently and uncontrollable sobs racked her body.

"It's all right, little one," he crooned, "it's all right. I never should have put you on that last rope." Misery filled the deep voice softly caressing her. "It's all my fault."

She desperately wanted to reassure him, tell him not to blame himself. It had happened because of her clumsiness, but she could find no voice through the sobs. Her arms were pinned to her sides by the tightly wrapped blanket and she couldn't touch him. She turned her face against his upper arm and continued to softly weep away her terror.

"Is Aunt Mercy going to be all right?" Esther whispered.

"Yes, she's going to be fine. She's not hurt, thank God, just badly frightened," Ben assured her. "And Saba, you were very brave to crawl under that wagon to help your aunt."

Saba flushed scarlet and murmured a thank-you.

At last, Mercy lay quiet. The sun heating the wool blanket began to penetrate the chill in her bones and she felt herself growing drowsy in Ben's arms. *It was worth nearly being killed to end up like this*, she thought.

"I'll carry Mercy down the hill and rest her in a sunny spot near the river," Ben said. "We've cleared the steepest part of the hill now, so Norah and Saba, if you want to come along, you can tend Mercy while Daniel and I finish bringing the wagon down."

Even through the layers of blanket, she felt the strength of his body holding her, felt the easy strides she had often admired. The last time she'd been carried like this, it had been her father who had wrapped her in a blanket and taken her into the house.

At that memory, she moved her face against Ben's sleeve until she could feel the scarf stretch taut against her cheek. Thank God for Norah's idea. The scarf had held fast through the ordeal and her scar, the permanent consequence of that other day, remained unexposed.

CHAPTER 6

BEN MADE HIMSELF SCARCE for the remainder of the trip. Mercy saw him only once after the incident on the hill—in Brookville, Indiana where they stopped to purchase their eighty acres of public land. Ben stood with Daniel then and offered his advice about the best parcel available. After that, he disappeared and she knew of his existence only by the blazes he marked on the trees to guide them. Finally, even that confirmation ended as the Wheelers came to the Michigan Road and no longer needed Ben's help.

Oddly enough, as long as Mercy could see evidences of Ben's continuing presence, she didn't think of him often. It was enough that he was somewhere nearby. But as soon as it seemed he had gone on his own way, thoughts of their brief encounter crowded all else from her mind. This both distressed and unnerved her. She found herself dwelling on those few moments by the river before she'd ended the tentative beginnings of their friendship with her foolish, albeit helpless, laughter. She relived and examined the half-numb emotions she'd felt in his arms as he'd cradled her with such tenderness after the accident.

At night when she curled into her blankets, she could still feel the strength of his arms about her, holding her to him, protecting her. She prayed constantly that by some miracle he would again clasp her to him in the same caring manner. She also decided that if he ever gave her the opportunity, she'd tell him as much. Then, if he turned his back on her, it would be for something she'd purposely done, not for an innocent laugh.

As he became more and more a part of her daydreams, he began invading her sleep as well. The dreams each night always ended the same. After some shared adventure, Ben would take her in his arms, kiss her gently on her eyelids, cheek, tip of the chin, tip of her nose, and finally firmly on the mouth. Then, before she could object, he'd untie the scarf to reveal the scar. She'd hold her breath, awaiting his reaction. However, instead of looking revolted, horrified, or sickened—emotions to which she'd grown accustomed—he would run the tips of his fingers over the crinkled skin, bend his head, and tenderly kiss the unsightly blemish.

"There," he'd say looking deep into her eyes, "it's well."

Without breaking their gaze, she'd reach her fingers to the familiar mark only to find it gone. Startled, she'd try to speak, but he would stop her. "Love heals all things," he would say before he kissed her again. Then, she would awaken to find her hand resting on the scar which was as ugly and disfiguring as before. Still, Ben had said it was "well" and that he loved her. So she would return to sleep with a warm glow replacing the cold hard knot that had been a part of her for so long.

This dream began occurring almost nightly, and Mercy looked forward to bedtime with an eagerness that was difficult to hide. In the daytime she worried about her reaction to Ben should she see him again.

With their imagined intimacy, however, she began to feel such a closeness to Ben that she gradually lost her awe of him.

Daniel kept insisting Ben would be directing them to their land, but when her brother stopped the wagon and called the family together, Mercy was skeptical. And, at his words, she was sure Ben was out of their lives forever.

"According to this map Ben drew for me," Daniel said, referring to a small sketch, "we're nearly there." The exultation in his voice was contagious and even the oxen quickened their steps.

The scale of the map was apparently not entirely accurate, however, for notwithstanding the faster pace, by late afternoon they still failed to reach the river where Ben's map showed he would be waiting.

Finally, Phelan, no longer able to tolerate what he considered "dallying about," charged on ahead and out of sight. Norah hadn't had time to worry about his whereabouts when he came running back, shouting, "Ben's waiting for us at the bridge!"

"A bridge! Good heavens, what is civilization doing here in the wilderness?" Norah gasped, but looked pleased with the information.

Mercy's heart gave an unrestricted bound at the thought of seeing Ben. He hadn't deserted them after all. She wondered if he looked as she had pictured him or if her imagination had embellished him out of all proportion.

They rounded a curve and Ben shouted a welcoming "Halloo!" and waved. Phelan couldn't contain his exuberance and raced to Ben's side.

Even from this distance, Mercy knew the woodsman to be as magnificent as she had remembered.

"Is our land here on the road?" Norah inquired.

"No, but we're only about two miles upstream," Daniel said, a note of regret in his voice. "Riverfront property was all taken closer, and you especially wanted to be on a river."

"Yes, I do that," Norah admitted. "Well, it's not so far back and once we get a trail marked, folks'll know how to find us." She seemed content.

"You made good time," Ben greeted them. "You'll be able to spend tonight on your own place."

"In our very own *house?*" Esther asked, and the laughter her question evoked eased the weariness of the travelers.

"I'm afraid it's going to be awhile before you have a firm roof over your head," Ben said. Then turning to Norah, he continued, "There's a fine place to build a half-face camp, though, so you can stop living out of the wagon."

"That *is* good news." She climbed down from the wagon. "I think I'll walk the rest of the way; I'd love to be able to say I started walking and I finished walking all the way to Indiana. Don't have to go into details about the in-between 'less I'm asked."

Norah's comments made Mercy smile. If someone did manage to break into a conversation enough to ask, Norah would smoothly gloss over the question, leaving the person satisfied without having revealed any more than she intended. Norah possessed a great talent for small talk which Mercy found herself greatly coveting at times. Perhaps if she had more practice she would become more adept, but when Mercy spoke, it was usually for specific reasons. She was most nearly herself when she was alone with Esther. In the midst of a group she became painfully tongue-tied.

Their land lay on the banks of the Big Blue, a lovely river "so full of fish, they positively beg to be removed from such crowded living conditions," Ben said.

Phelan pulled out his knife and cut a willow. "In that case, I'm obliged to save them from further discomfort," he said with a grin.

Ben produced some line and a hook from his

pocket. "Tie this on your pole and I'll dig some fresh worms. By the time we get a fire hot, you'll have a mess of redeye to tempt a king's palate."

Daniel drove the wagon into a good-sized clearing and began unhitching the teams.

It took a few minutes for the reality of their arrival to settle in and then Norah, hands placed on her rounded hips, asked, "Where are the trees?" Joy and disbelief took turns displaying themselves across her wide features.

"Looks to have been a heavy wind or small fire years ago and cleared a spot," Ben answered. "I knew these cleared acres were here. I hoped this was what you'd bought."

"Then I owe you double for your service," Daniel said and reached for his money pouch.

Ben held up his hand in rejection of Daniel's offer. "Don't owe me anything except help when it comes time to build my cabin."

"I'll certainly do that and more, if I'm able."

As they went about setting up camp, it took all Mercy's self-discipline to keep her eyes down. She didn't dare look up for she didn't know what she would do if Ben were to catch her watching him. She found her bedroll in the wagon and carried it to a secluded spot a bit farther from the family than usual. She knelt and began untying it when Ben's familiar bass voice washed over her.

"Unless you've had a falling out with your family, I think it would be safer to sleep nearer the fire."

Startled and before she could regain control, her eyes flew up and met Ben's gaze. Her mouth went cotton-dry and she could feel a flush rise from her throat and color her face. With trembling fingers she attempted to gather the bedding.

"Here, let me help," Ben said, kneeling down beside her.

All the clever witty things she'd thought up to say if

such a moment should ever occur vanished, and she appeared to be struck dumb.

"What do you think of this spot?" he asked.

"I .. I .. uh .. like it just fine," she stammered. *Oh please, God—help me get my thoughts together before he thinks I'm dimwitted!*

He helped her to her feet and walked beside her carrying the bed. "If you don't object, I think this is a safer place." He dropped to the ground and began spreading the blankets out in a smooth grassy spot. "Have you been sleeping so far from the fire?" The edge of concern revealed in his words surprised her.

Taking a deep breath, she said, "No. I had the mistaken notion that on our own land, it would be safe."

A low chuckle rumbled from his chest. "The creatures don't know it's your land. They still think they have first claim and will until we get a cabin and a palisade fence built."

Mercy could feel his eyes full on her and she had to look at him. Had to let him know she returned the caring. She knelt beside him and reached for the corner of a quilt. Slowly, she raised her eyes until they locked with his. Tonight his eyes shimmered a soft golden brown—the same warm color they'd held when he'd looked deep into her eyes just before he settled her beneath the large friendly sycamore, that night after he'd carried her down the hill.

Her world grew silent now except for the sound of her heart pounding in her ears. She was aware only of Ben. The thick muscles of his arms and shoulders— she remembered the feel of them wrapped around her. She felt the strength flow from him. His beard hid his neck, but not his full, generous mouth. It was open now in a slight smile, revealing strong square teeth. There was a small scratch on one cheek and without thinking, she reached up and touched it.

"Come to the river and let me tend your cut," she

said, her voice soft and sure as in her dreams. Only now she was awake and this was really happening.

"It's nothing."

"Could be, though, if it's not washed. Dry blood's caked in your beard."

Her hand still rested on his cheek. Slowly, he gathered her hand in his and drew it to his lips. There he placed a kiss on each fingertip and gently folded her tingling fingers until they curved over his. "After supper."

She could only nod in agreement for she knew no words would issue from her trembling lips.

He rose and left her side and she grew instantly cold. She had been unaware of the warmth she had drawn from him. Now she found her cape and slipped it on as protection against the disappearing sun. It would soon set and the mists would begin rising from the river. The fire would feel very welcome in a short time.

"Mercy, would you see to Esther?" Norah called, shattering the spell in which Mercy was still cloaked.

Quickly, Mercy descended to earth. These exquisite moments could be examined in minute detail later. "Right away," she answered and jumped to her feet. Looking about she could see Saba, but no Esther. *They must be playing hide-and-seek.* Watching a few minutes more, Mercy heard Esther's shrill excited giggle as Saba found her. Gathering her skirts, Mercy ran across the grass to where the girls were playing.

"Isn't it wonderful to have open ground and see the sky?" Saba asked.

"It is a great blessing," Mercy answered. But she considered Saba's willingness to talk with her an even greater blessing. Ever since the incident with the wheel Saba had been very considerate of her. Never mind that she wanted to mother Mercy. The fact that Saba acknowledged Mercy's existence was a far step from the cold disregard of the past.

"Want to play?" Esther asked.

"I surely do. Why else do you think I came?"

"Then it's your turn to be 'it,' " Esther announced. She loved to play hide-and-seek, but she much preferred the hiding to the seeking.

It was nearly dark before Norah called them all to supper. Ben and Daniel created a makeshift table by splitting a log in half, and Norah spread it with a cloth. She even unpacked some of her dishes.

"We're going to celebrate our first meal on our new land," she said.

Daniel read from the biblical account of the exodus—where the children of Israel were led safely out of the wilderness. Then he gave a stirring prayer of thanksgiving for their own safe arrival *into* the wilderness. Supper was corn bread and fresh rabbit, fried crisp on the outside and mouthwateringly tender inside.

"A right pleasing meal, my dear," Daniel said.

"And made the more festive with such an elegant table," Ben's teeth gleamed white against his beard.

Norah glowed with the unaccustomed praise. "It *is* good to have my things out of the trunks. There were times when I wasn't sure I'd ever see them spread again."

"You were a good pioneer, dear. I'm proud of all of you." Daniel, leaning back against the wagon wheel, lavished looks of affection on them all.

"You have a fine family."

Mercy didn't trust herself to glance at Ben, noting the pain that flickered across his face.

He stood and stretched. "If you'll excuse me, I seem to have run crosswise of a haw tree. Need to do a little doctoring."

"Anything I can do?" Norah offered.

"It's just a scratch. A bit of washing with some good lye soap will do the job." He started toward the river with fluid strides, making no sound.

Without a word, Mercy rose, filled a small kettle with hot water from the large pot over the fire, gathered soap and a towel, and followed him. She could feel questioning eyes burning into her back and knew she'd have some explaining to do when she returned.

Ben was waiting for her at the top of the riverbank. Wordlessly, he took the kettle from her and captured her hand. The bank was steep and they hadn't had time to build a proper trail down, so she relied on him to steady her over the boulders and dead logs flung by spring floods high onto the sloping sides of the river.

A full moon appeared, lighting their way and reflecting off the water. "Almost as light as day," Ben observed as he placed the kettle in the sand by the river and sat on a log.

"Almost," Mercy said as she came to stand in front of him. She was exactly as tall as he now and could look him straight in the eye. In her dreams, she had stood like this with him many a time; it now felt very natural and comfortable. She lifted his hat and set it on the log. "Tip your head up a bit to catch the light."

He did as she bid him and she leaned closer to examine the cut.

"Hmmm—this wound doesn't seem as innocent as I first thought." She dampened the towel in the hot water and added a generous amount of soap. Gently but thoroughly, she sponged away the dried blood. Now the jagged tear, free from its camouflage, stood boldly against the tan of his cheek, snaking its way down into the beard. "You're lucky it didn't grab your eye as well," she observed.

"How bad is it?"

She rinsed out the towel. "Only appears deep in one spot. Don't see any fresh blood. Is there much pain?"

"Stings a bit from the cleaning."

"I'll put a hot compress on it for a few minutes to draw out the soreness."

Mercy folded the towel and laid it across his cheek. As she stood there holding it in place, she felt his arm go around her shoulders.

"Sting's gone. It'll be fine now."

He took the towel from her hand and laid it on the log, then drew her close, her forehead resting against his cheek. He wrapped his other arm around her until she was completely enfolded.

"I've wanted to do this again, ever since I held you after the accident," he murmured, his voice a low, pulsing throb. "Dreamed of it as I rode in the woods. Couldn't stand being near you for the wanting of it."

So he *had* thought of her. Had dreams of her as she had of him.

"Oh, Ben," she whispered and wound her arms around his neck. "Even in my terror as I clung to the wagon wheel, I drew strength from your caring. Knew you were the reason I survived with so little shock. I've—I've dreamed of you in the nights since." She tipped her face to his and watched his eyes play over her features.

"You are the most beautiful woman I've ever seen," he breathed. "Someday I intend to paint you." And then he bent his head to her upturned face. She closed her eyes and felt his lips on her eyelids, her cheek, her chin, the tip of her nose. Her lips trembled as he claimed them at last. Clear crystal chimes shimmered in her ears, resounding in her heart. She *wasn't* doomed to live alone. God had sent her a man—a perfect man—to love her and marry her and father her children. She drifted, weightless, completely happy for the first time in her life.

Then, without warning, he ripped his mouth from hers, wrenched her arms from his neck, and thrust her from him.

"No!" he growled, low and frightening. "No!"

He left her, trembling and disoriented, and stalked to the river's edge. She wanted to flee, but this time she knew she'd done nothing—nothing at all to merit such treatment. Anger filled the places love had occupied and she raced to stand beside him. "What is the matter with you?" she demanded, stamping her feet. "I laughed the first time—an innocent reaction to my delight—but it upset you unreasonably. Now . . . ? You owe me an explanation."

His breath came in ragged gulps. He continued to stare out across the water, his arms hanging loosely at his sides. Beads of sweat stood on his brow and his tongue licked a coating of moisture over his lips. At last his breathing steadied.

"You're right." He paused as though groping for the words. "The first time wasn't your fault and neither was this. I had no right to encourage you to come to the river with me—to take advantage of you."

"Why not? I wanted to come, and I wanted what happened to happen. I've dreamed for days that it would. Prayed that it would." And now she had come to the hard part—the part she had to know and barely had the courage to ask. "Is it my face?"

"I told you, you're the most beautiful woman I've ever seen."

"But you haven't seen the other half of my face. It isn't beautiful. It's horribly ugly." There, she'd said it. She started to untie the scarf that held the ruffle in place.

He sensed what she was doing and grabbed her wrist. "Stop! I don't want to see it."

Mercy crumpled inside. It *was* her face. It would always be her face. Somehow, she'd thought Ben was different, but he wasn't. All men were the same. They could not tolerate imperfection in the women they chose to honor with their presence. She turned to run, but he held her arm in a vice-like grip.

"It isn't your face," he repeated. "It's me—me. I'm a coward. I don't want to be hurt again." He loosened the grip slightly. "Will you stay and hear me out?"

She nodded and he led the way back to the log. This time she sat beside him and they both stared into the river. His voice came cold and flat.

"I had a wonderful wife and four beautiful children—nearly the copy of Daniel's own children. Esther reminds me constantly of my youngest. Genny and I had some fine acreage in eastern Pennsylvania and I taught in a small college. Life was good. Then the fever struck and took them all. I wasn't alone in my loss. Nearly wiped out the whole town. Left a few of us to suffer the losses and do the burying. I vowed never to let that kind of hurt into my life again."

Mercy wanted to wrap him in her arms, croon away the anguish that rose in his voice, help him know life could be good again. She reached out to touch him, but felt his rejection, strong and violent, though she laid no hand on him.

"I made a bad mistake offering to bring you folks here. But I can't leave you now until you're properly settled. I'll move on as soon as I'm satisfied, though."

"Where will you go?"

"Build me a cabin to get by the winter. Likely travel west come spring. There's always new country. Don't ever run out of country."

"You can't do that for the rest of your life. You have to care about something or someone."

"That's where you're wrong. Caring hurts, and I can live without more of that."

"You mean, if you could begin your life again, you'd never marry and have a family? Never make beautiful memories? Or wipe them out and pretend they didn't exist? I don't believe that." She lowered her voice. "What keeps you going? What do you think about when you're all alone?"

His broad shoulders slumped forward, his face buried in his hands. "My children—and Genny."

"Then why are you denying yourself the possibility of other children—another Genny—or someone who could love you just as much?" She surprised herself. It was not like Mercy to be so forward.

He gazed past her, into the woods—lost in some dark world of his own. Crickets began chirping their night song, and the mist rose from the river like a veil, filtering the moonbeams, turning them to pale gold lace. And still he sat.

Mercy didn't know whether to say more or simply slip away. He would likely not even notice if she were to leave. Still, she couldn't bring herself to desert him in his grief.

Haltingly he spoke, breaking the heavy silence. "This may not make any sense to you, but when I kissed you a bit ago, your face gradually faded away and it was Genny's face I saw—Genny I was kissing. Do you want that kind of love? Because that's all I have to offer you." His eyes shadowed until they felt the full measure of the great sorrow he still bore.

She shook her head slowly. "No . . . I couldn't bear that. I wouldn't take away your memories— you'll always have that much of the family you lost. But I need to know that those memories have taken their rightful place—in the past. I can't compete with a memory that is more real to you than I am." She paused and swallowed hard. "Thank you, Ben, for being honest with me."

Mercy started to turn away, but she couldn't go without touching him once more and so she placed her hands against his cheeks. His beard bristled against her palms.

"I do love you, Ben Tasker. I've never loved anyone before you, and it isn't likely I shall love anyone after. If you can leave your past behind you, I'll be waiting."

She reached up on tiptoe and kissed him, not caring for the moment if it were Genny he was seeing, for this kiss must last Mercy for the rest of her life.

CHAPTER 7

MERCY SLEPT POORLY. For the first time she dreamed of the axle winding her into the turning wheel. She awoke in a cold sweat while it was yet dark, alone.

It was a long time before she grew calm enough to drift back to sleep, and so morning found her tired and short-tempered. She kept thinking of all the things she had said to Ben last night. She must have been mad, completely insane. And how was she going to face him this morning?

After her morning prayers, Mercy felt some better and determined not to brood more. There was not time now. Fretting would have to wait until later in the day.

"We're going to build the half-face camp against that big fallen tree," Saba said, pointing up the slope. Papa says we need to gather limbs and twigs to hang over the two long poles he and Ben are going to put into the forks of those young hickories. They'll serve as the walls. Come, Aunt Mercy."

Taking Esther's hand, Saba led the way to the edge of the forest where they gathered armloads of branches. This activity took most of the morning, but by noon they had a fine shelter.

"The camp's open in the front," Esther observed.

"That's why it's called a half-face camp," Phelan informed her. "At night we'll hang skins and blankets over the opening and keep a fire burning outside to scare away any curious animals."

Norah called the family together and Mercy insisted on serving the dinner. It would be easier, with Ben so near.

"It's surely nice to sit at a table again like a lady," Norah commented.

By concentrating on the stew, Mercy was able to keep her hand from trembling as she placed Ben's bowl in front of him. After the meal, the men disappeared. After Mercy washed the dishes, she wandered up to the half-face camp where Norah supervised the making of the beds. The children were gathering piles of green leafy twigs to ease the hardness of the ground, and Norah covered these with skins she'd brought from Virginia.

"Do you know where Daniel and Ben are?"

"Gone to visit our neighbors," Norah replied. "Let them know we've arrived and learn about the land." She paused and cast a glance at the sun. "Should be back soon. Promised not to be gone after dark."

The sun had slid over the horizon, however, when the two men returned. "You both look about ready to explode," Norah observed.

"We met Anne and William Franklin, our closest neighbors. Told us they'd arrange a cabin raising soon as we're ready."

"Oh, Daniel, that's just wonderful!" Norah said. "We'll have our cabin lots faster than we ever dreamed."

After supper, Norah led the way to the site she'd chosen for the cabin. Facing west, there would be a clear view of the river. We'll plant a bluegrass lawn all the way to the river bank. There are just the right number of trees left standing. With the rosebushes and the fruit trees, we'll soon be right at home," she said with a laugh and a sweep of her arm.

And then Ben will leave—for good. I'll never see him again, sighed Mercy. *Funny, how the same thing can make one person deliriously happy and bring the end of the world to another* . Mercy slipped away from the happy group and cried out her loneliness on the riverbank.

For the next few days Ben, Daniel, and Phelan chopped trees from sunup to sundown, pausing only long enough to wolf down cold rabbit stew and cornpone. Saba and Mercy carried their meals to them in the woods. Mercy tried to arrange it so Saba took Ben his dinner, but near the end of the second week, as Norah handed Mercy the pail, she said, "Saba's already gone with Daniel's dinner. Ben's working down by the river."

Had Norah done that deliberately? Mercy wondered. There was no avoiding an encounter with him now, and her heart pulsed erratically as she hurried on her errand. She could hear Ben's axe thud against a tree trunk. A slight breeze caught the top branches and the trunk swayed into the wind, then crashed onto the forest floor just after Mercy stepped into Ben's line of view. A look of surprise crossed his face momentarily, then it became a blank, neither welcoming nor forbidding.

"I .. I . . . I've brought your dinner," she faltered and handed the pail to him.

He nodded and sat down to eat.

"Daniel says you've nearly enough logs to start the cabin."

Without replying or looking up, he continued to eat. *At least there's nothing wrong with his hearing,* she thought sarcastically.

While she waited for him to finish, Mercy wandered about, inspecting the heavy timbers stacked in piles, ready to be dragged by oxen to the cabin site. Ben had felled an unbelievable number of trees by himself—more even than Daniel and Phelan. She wondered if he knew that, or if he cared. He seemed not to care about much these days. She hadn't seen him drawing in the dirt for days—not since their evening at the river.

The spoon clanked in the empty pail and she started at the noise. Ben handed her the pail, stood, and shouldered the axe to begin again. She sighed and stepped carefully over the branch-littered ground. Behind her she heard the axe slam violently into the trunk. It's harshness jarred her and she spun around.

Ben's hand still clung to the handle, but he looked over his shoulder, full at her. His eyes squinted, though there was no sun. "Thanks, Mercy," he said softly, and turned to his work.

The gesture left her more confused than ever. Saba would take Ben his dinner in the future, Mercy vowed to herself.

By the end of the week, they had enough logs to build the cabin Norah wanted—two rooms, one with a loft, and a front porch. Daniel rode out with the word and came back to say the log cabin raising would begin Friday.

"Anne says not to worry about food," he anticipated Norah's concern. "Everybody will bring plenty, enough for the two days it'll take."

"Two days!" Norah exclaimed. "Are you saying in two days we'll have our new home?"

"That's what Will says and he's helped build many a cabin."

Norah's face beamed with the anticipation of having her own house again.

Mercy looked for Ben, but he had disappeared. Her

heart lay like a stone in her breast. While he'd only once acknowledged her presence since the night by the river, she had often felt his eyes upon her. Even these little crumbs made each new morning worthwhile, and each night a time for imagining a miracle in which he would tell her Genny was at last a dim memory and she, Mercy, was real for him.

The settlers for twenty miles up and down the river arrived early Friday. While one group worked on the house, another worked a distance from the cabin, putting up the barn, with room for horses, oxen, and cows. A third group dug holes and built a palisade fence which enclosed the barn and about five acres of pasture. The animals could graze free by day, but the fence would protect them from the varmints that roamed at night.

For the next two days, Mercy ran from group to group with food and drink. When at last she fell into bed at the end of the week, she was too tired to do more than say her prayers, anticipating the Sabbath to come, when the neighbors who had stayed the night, would gather to worship. With no church building, no preacher, and folks living so far apart, a real meeting wasn't held often. Because such an occasion was rare, it was all the more precious.

Dressed in their best clothes, the men and boys sat on logs around the makeshift tables spread under the trees and visited while the women and girls prepared the meal. The arrival of the itinerate preacher in early afternoon signaled the beginning of dinner.

The tables groaned with the trenchers and baskets heaped with good things to eat—baked fish, roast beef and onions, fried chicken, leg of pork and turnips, cheeses, breads, puddings and fresh wild strawberries. The young girls followed with pitchers of punch, cold tea, and buttermilk.

When the bountiful meal was finished, tables were

cleared and the logs rolled into rows, ready for the service. Mercy sat at the back and tried to concentrate on the preaching, but she was distracted by thoughts of Ben. Finally, she spotted him, leaning against a beech tree at the edge of the clearing. Constant, saddled and bridled, and the pony, packed for traveling, grazed nearby. Soon—soon he would be leaving.

As they rose to sing the closing hymn, she glanced again in Ben's direction. His spot beneath the tree was vacant, and the horses were gone. A lump rose in her throat, choking off the words of "When We Gather at the River." How could she stand here in the midst of these people who were singing so joyously, when there was no song in her heart?

She felt numb, empty. the real Mercy Wheeler had vanished, leaving no clue as to her whereabouts, but the imposter carried on flawlessly. Not one person guessed the truth. Not even Esther. Only Mercy knew.

CHAPTER 8

AS SOON AS THE WHEELERS WERE SETTLED into their new home, Daniel and some of the near neighbors went to help Ben build his winter cabin. With the men away, Anne Franklin arranged a blackberry-picking excursion.

"There's a large berry patch close to the settlement that shouldn't be any danger from Indians or bears," she said. "Will does hate picking so I try to go when he's not around. Otherwise, he feels he has to go along to protect us. In ten years the most danger we've faced was when a bear cub upset a hive of bees." She chuckled at the memory and convinced a reluctant Norah that it would make a nice outing.

Soon after sunrise a few days later, Anne and her three children, Jim, Tom, and Grace, arrived at the Wheelers' river landing in their large gum log canoe. In the mist rising from the water they appeared like apparitions floating silently across the placid surface.

"We're ready!" Norah hailed them.

Esther frisked about the canoe like a new puppy.

She saw her friend Grace, who, at the knowledgeable age of eight, was still young enough to enjoy childish play.

"Just think," Esther said, her excited little voice ringing through the morning-quiet forest, "we get to spend a whole day together, and we don't have to work at all!"

"If you think picking blackberries isn't work, then you've never picked," Jim said, and easily swung the Wheelers' empty deerskin sacks, picking gourds, and lunch into the boat.

Mercy lifted Esther in beside Grace and then climbed aboard. When everyone was settled, Tom and Phelan pushed the canoe free from the gripping sand and tumbled inside, and Jim poled the boat into the swift-moving current.

With Norah and Anne chatting happily and the children bubbling with anticipation, Mercy was free to sit quietly with her own thoughts. It surprised her how comfortable she had grown to feel around these people. Living in Indiana was pleasant—as long as she didn't think about Ben.

When he left to build his own cabin, he'd made it very clear he didn't plan to return, and he issued no invitations for any of the Wheelers to visit. But despite her best efforts, he constantly slipped into her thoughts.

Mercy was jarred from her thinking about not thinking about Ben by the bump of the canoe as Jim nosed it into the bank.

"Everybody out!" He led the way into the woods and, carrying their lunches and berrying sacks, the others followed to the thicket of blackberry bushes.

The picking commenced at a rapid rate, each picker filling the gourds and emptying them into the sacks. The dark juice stained their fingers, and the fragrance rising from the fresh berries was nearly overwhelming in its tempting sweetness. They resisted, however, and by noon about half the sacks were filled, and the hungry crew fell on a lunch of whole-wheat bread and cold venison. Dessert was fresh crisp sugar cookies baked for the occasion. Their appetites sated, they sat in the cool shade, told stories, and asked riddles. Mercy found herself included, a circumstance she rarely enjoyed.

"Well," Jim declared, "we've rested long enough. If we don't get busy, there will still be unpicked berries when we run out of daylight. That would be a terrible waste."

Laughing, they returned to their picking with renewed vigor.

"If we stop now," Jim suggested around mid-afternoon, "we'll have plenty of daylight left to get home by." He produced a crude skid made for transporting the sacks to the river. "You children play some games while we load these bags in the boat," he said with exaggerated importance..

When the skid was loaded, the three women and Jim started pulling it down the path to the river. Just before the trail led out of sight, Norah turned to Mercy. "I have an uneasy feeling. Would you mind staying near the children? It would relieve my mind if you did."

Strange! It was usually Mercy who had such feelings, but today she felt nothing. "Very well. I don't mind."

By the time she returned to the clearing the youngsters were well into a game of "Ring Around a Rosey." Mercy made herself comfortable on a fallen log from which she had a good view of the clearing.

Finally they turned to the favorite, "Hide-and-Seek," hiding behind trees at the edge of the clearing and in dense clumps of bushes. Phelan and Tom climbed some of the smaller trees, but the hollow trees were best of all and were eagerly sought by everyone. The clearing was small and before long the game grew dull.

"I always get caught first," Esther complained. "I'm tired of being 'it.'"

"I'll take your place," Saba volunteered.

"Aunt Mercy, can't we hide a little farther in the woods?"

After considering the childish plea, Mercy agreed, on one condition. "Only if you stay very close by. You mustn't venture so far that we can't find you.

Of course, that was the idea exactly, and so Mercy kept her eyes glued to the child as Saba began counting.

"Fifty-nine, sixty . . . "

A shrill cry pierced the air.

Mercy leaped to her feet and pushed her way through the tangle of bushes into a small clearing beyond. On the opposite side of the open space, some twenty or thirty yards away, Esther stood frozen, her hands outstretched, staring at a huge old sycamore tree. The base of the tree was obscured by underbrush, and Mercy could see nothing from her vantage point.

She raced across the opening, but stopped short as she reached a point where she could look into the hollow at the root of the ancient tree. An enormous bear emerged from the opening and started slowly toward Esther, who was too frightened to move.

"Run, Esther! Run for your life!" Mercy screamed and rushed toward the bear, trying to distract him.

Throwing sticks, rocks, clods—anything she could get her hands on, she attacked the huge animal, shouting at the top of her lungs. But it had eyes only for Esther, and continued its determined rolling gait directly for her.

"Run, Esther! Run!"

This last shout penetrated the fear-induced trance and Esther tore off into the trees, with the bear crashing through the underbrush after her.

Mercy followed, crying hysterically, while in her

89

terror, Esther fled deeper and deeper into the darkening woods. With night coming on, Mercy knew they would soon be hopelessly lost.

Searching desperately, she found a stout stick and taking a short cut around a clump of underbrush, came close enough to hear the short, impatient grunts as the great black creature lumbered steadily on after Esther. Gathering all her strength, Mercy lunged at the huge animal, thrusting the blunt end of the stick viciously into the bear's side. With a furious growl, it turned on Mercy, its sharp glistening teeth snapping only a few feet away. Heedless of the danger, she slammed the stick over the great dish-shaped head.

The bear shook off the blow as if it were a mosquito bite and focused its luminous green eyes on Mercy. Poised to receive the fatal swipe of a huge paw, Mercy found herself concentrating on one of the creature's ears which hung limp and shredded. Obviously, he had not survived all his battles unscathed. Recovering her senses, she bashed him again, this time on his snout. He let out a great roar of pain. Without looking back, she scrambled over a large fallen log as the bear came growling and grunting at her heels.

Then, to her horror she heard Esther scream, "Aunt Mercy!" and turned around to see the bear again making its resolute way toward the little girl.

This time Esther needed no urging to run. All Mercy could hear were Esther's departing screams and the crashing of the fickle bear in pursuit.

"Esther!" she called over and over as she fought her way deeper into the woods, struggling over giant fallen logs and snagging her skirts on branches. After tripping numerous times over roots, at last, she lay sobbing with exhaustion and fear, unaware of the gathering darkness and fine drizzle of rain.

Finally, thoughts of Esther drove Mercy to pull herself up and plod onward, repeatedly calling the child's name until she grew too hoarse to be heard.

Intense gripping panic stole over her, and she faded in and out of reality. Losing touch with the real world frightened her. How was she going to help Esther if she couldn't keep her wits about her?

She heard wolves howling in the distance and the thought that they might be following Esther drove Mercy almost frantic. In her hysteria, Mercy's thoughts rambled, became disjointed, and her imagination conjured up all sorts of horrors. She pictured unseen cliffs down which the little girl could tumble, bottomless bogs and caves waiting to swallow her, and worst of all, the flop-eared bear lurking to pounce, or Indians lying in ambush ready to snatch the child and carry her off to a distant camp. On and on Mercy went, stumbling in terror through the demon-filled night.

At daybreak, she found herself near a wide slow-flowing river. Standing confused, exhausted, grief-stricken, she staggered to the water's edge. There, she sank slowly to her knees. How she yearned for the comfort of prayer, but sometime in the night she had lost touch with everything including God. she felt cut off, detached. "Oh, God! Where are You?" she cried. But the warm secure feeling she always received when she sought His help was denied her and she knelt, cold and desolate.

With a cry of deep anguish, she fell prostrate on the ground, too overcome even to cry. Dry-eyed, she stared unseeing along the shoreline, her mind numb and unfunctioning.

Then, an unnatural object bobbed in the water, half-hidden by the bushes overhanging the bank. She blinked and came awake. The morning mist obscured the outline, but as near as she could tell, it was a canoe. Before she could gather strength to rise, a tall figure dressed in buckskin with fringed leggins emerged from the woods carrying something over his shoulder.

Ben! She wanted to laugh and shout his name, to praise God for sending him to find Esther. How had he known? It didn't matter. By some miracle he knew of Mercy's prayers and pleadings.

"*Ben!*" She was calling at the top of her voice. Why didn't he look in her direction? Why couldn't he see her? She called out again, then realized she was only making gurgling sounds quickly dispelled by the running river.

The man approached the canoe and, dumping his burden inside, looked warily from side to side before he bent and untied the boat. Moving stealthily but quickly, he stepped into the canoe, turned to look once more, and picked up his paddle.

He had no beard! An Indian! Her scalp tingled with the knowledge.

Seeing nothing, he pushed away from the bank and glided silently into the current.

"Esther!" Mercy's scream ended in a hoarse croak. Struggling to her feet, she staggered over the rocks, stepping on her skirt and tearing another long rip in the already tattered ruins. She tripped over an unseen branch and sprawled headlong onto the sandy bank, burying her face in the ground. She sat up and spit out the sand and moldy leaves. Gagging, she crawled to the river and scooped up water to rinse her mouth. The water in her hands turned bright red from cuts she had not noticed before.

She tried to stand, stepping on her dragging skirts again, and fell. A low moan punctuated her agony. This wretched skirt had constantly hampered her searching. Intense unreasoning anger boiled up, and she ripped off the offending garment and flung it away. Regaining her footing, she staggered along the narrow strip of beach until it disappeared into eroded tree roots and the bank grew too steep to climb. Standing with water lapping over her ankles, she watched the rising mist swallow up both man and canoe.

"Esther," she sobbed. "Esther. . . ." The ground rose slowly to meet her, and Mercy passed into blessed oblivion.

CHAPTER 9

Mercy could bear the crowded cabin no longer and, under cover of darkness, she retreated to the sanctuary of the Conestoga Wagon. Here, however, there were the night sounds—the sustained "whooos" of the long-eared owl, its barred relative's distinctive rhythmic call, occasional distant howls of wolves—all driving spears of terror through Mercy's heart. The wild creatures seemed undaunted by the red glow of the fire the men had set on the hillside to guide Esther if, by some miracle, she should be able to see it and find her way home. Instead, the beasts prowled their nocturnal rounds, giving no notice that a little girl was lost—or worse.

Mercy started at the far-off wail of a panther. Why, oh why, couldn't she remember? When Esther needed her most, Mercy could help her least. And where was God when she needed Him? Mercy raged inside, but nothing broke through the dense black void of her memory.

It had been like this when Jim found her. Summoned by blasts on the great hunting horn, the closest neighbors had rushed to the Wheelers' place. More people continued to arrive during the day as the news passed up and down the river. Though their company gave Norah comfort it was Mercy they fixed with their stares.

Each new arrival asked the same questions, and Norah told the story over again. For Mercy, each repetition was as empty of memories as the first time. It brought no pictures to her mind, no sounds, no smells. She concentrated intently, hoping she could remember even a small detail, but nothing surfaced.

Not understanding, the smallest children played happily, but the older girls stood quietly near their mothers inside the cabin. The men and boys who arrived too late to make the hastily assembled search party stood outside on the porch in a tight knot, making men's talk, telling tales of others they knew to be lost. There was a sense of excitement in their tired voices, but now and again when a father thought he was unobserved, he cast an anxious eye on his youngest.

At the first drops of rain pelting the canvas top, a violent spasm wracked Mercy's body, and she bit her knuckles to strangle the scream threatening to escape. She'd been told it rained last night, too.

Esther! Poor bedraggled mite—somewhere out in that dark woods. She couldn't take off her soggy clothes and snuggle into the warm dry loft bed tonight.

Mercy couldn't bear to think that Esther wasn't alive. Couldn't imagine life without the little tyke who was likely the closest Mercy would ever come to having a child of her own. These thoughts and more skittered across her benumbed brain, lingering only long enough to add to the already overwhelming mountain of grief and guilt, then vanishing, half-formed and unremembered.

The sound of muffled footsteps interrupted Mercy's

agonizing as the sodden tracking team entered the clearing, straggling back through the darkness to the cabin, their torches extinguished by the rain. In the light streaming from the cabin door, she recognized Ben. She hadn't known until now if word had reached him.

He stood for a moment, framed in the doorway, shoulders slumped and deep lines of exhaustion chiseled in his face. There, Mercy read the shock of Esther's loss, knew his suffering in the distant confused look in his eyes. He had been as incapable of helping Esther as she.

The sight of Ben's pain brought a sudden comprehension of the message he had tried to give her that night by the river—that one doesn't ever quite recover from the loss of loved ones. Mercy hadn't experienced such a loss until now—hadn't known the knifing hurt, the helplessness.

Norah came from the cabin and went to stand by Daniel. "Any word from Judah Tull?" he asked, his voice flat and dull. "Promised he'd be right over with his dogs."

"None yet," someone answered. "But don't fret yourself. Judah may be a might slow gettin' around, but don't nobody know these woods like him. Him and his dogs has found many a lost-un safe and brung 'em out."

These remarks served to ease the tension and, by the time Judah's hounds bayed their arrival, the atmosphere in the Wheeler cabin had lightened considerably.

"We'll find yore young'un come first light, ma'am!" called a coarse voice from outside the cabin.

"You will iffen she hain't been kilt by that big old bear or some other wild critter," moaned a high voice from within.

Mercy gasped at the woman's insensitive response and hoped her sister-in-law hadn't heard.

"After you men eat, there's room in the barn to bed down," Norah invited. "Got plenty of quilts and there's fresh hay spread. We appreciate your kindness." Even in the face of this horror, Norah could see to her guests comfort, Mercy marveled. How could she, when it seemed for Mercy that she could never again close her eyes in sleep.

She couldn't bring herself to climb to the loft, so she curled into a quilt inside the shelter of the wagon and spent the night, staring into the dark, misty forest.

At dawn the searchers stirred and bolted down their breakfast. Armed with rifles and clubs, the band of men, led by Judah Tull and his hounds, slogged across the rain-soaked clearing and into the woods.

"Pray God they find her." Lines of grief and weariness were etched sharply into Norah's face as she stood with the women at the cabin door.

Saba came and put her arm about her mother's shoulder and Norah leaned heavily against the young girl, burying her face in her daughter's hair. But Mercy sat alone in her grief with no one to comfort her or offer her hope.

When the searchers returned that night, all they had seen was a child's footprint by a stream. A blast from the horn had brought everyone to the spot, and they tramped out the sign before it could be determined if it belonged to Esther. The third day—nothing.

By the morning of the following day, Ben set himself in charge. "In three days all we have found is one footprint we can't be sure belonged to Esther. Dashing about helter-skelter is no way to proceed. I suggest we leave the dogs home and make a planned search."

Judah Tull made it plain he wasn't pleased by gathering his dogs and storming off for home. But when Ben presented his plan, the men nodded their agreement, and began moving to collect their supplies.

Mercy, filled with the frustration of inaction, gathered her courage and approached Ben. "Won't you need all the people you can get to help in the search?"

He looked down at her through expressionless eyes. "Yes, we will—all the men and boys. I'm afraid you wouldn't be much good in the woods. If you're volunteering, I'd say you're needed far more here to help with women's work."

His words, steady and unemotional, nonetheless flayed her spirit like the lash of a whip. Ben regarded her for a long moment. Then, with a curt nod, he dismissed her and rejoined the men. When everything was to his satisfaction, he slung his rifle over his shoulder and the searchers moved silently into the forest again.

Mercy turned to the cabin. Since Esther's disappearance the women had studiously avoided her and she retired to a corner, listening to their talk—the wives and the widows and the blossoming young ones—all bonded by the loves they had known or were yet to know. Mercy didn't belong. It had ever been so.

As the day wore on, the speculations as to Esther's whereabouts grew more gruesome.

"My granny was lost for four days once," said one. "She allowed as how even a growed woman will run 'til she's fallin'-down tired—like Mercy when Jim found her."

All eyes sought Mercy in the dark corner where she sat snapping beans. She recoiled as though from a blow, so palpable were the stares.

It wasn't that they blamed her, Mercy knew. Saba, Norah, and Anne had explained what they had seen and heard. But Mercy's numbed brain reeled with the effort of remembering, and the events that had transpired remained shrouded in darkness.

As the old woman's story continued, Mercy's heart began to beat like a wild thing.

"The brain's befogged," the woman droned on, "and a body cain't even recognize ground they's tromped every day. Thinks the tracks is someone else's, and if a sound is heard, she runs and hides. Jes' ain't human no more. Now, if a growed woman acts that way, how's a babe like Esther to fare?" She turned mournful eyes on Norah. "You get 'er back, and she won't ever be the same."

Norah paled and Mercy clapped her hands over her ears to block out the hideous tale, but the insensitive creature paid no heed to the distress she was causing.

"Sometimes it's a good thing if you don't find a lost 'un." The storyteller wiped her eyes. "If they're gone too long, I'd as soon see 'em dead and buried. Better that than the not knowin', and the awful waitin' and wonderin'."

Oh, no! Mercy wanted to scream. *Esther can't be dead!* As long as she wasn't found, there was hope. Unable to sit and listen longer, Mercy slipped from her corner and went to Norah. "She's wrong, Norah. I know she's wrong, and I'm sorry she's saying these hurtful things. Someone should have stopped her." Mercy paused. "*I* should have stopped her."

For a moment the two women clasped each other in their mutual pain, then Mercy walked from the room and into the forest nearest the cabin. She wished she could know if the horn had sounded a message yet today. She knelt to pray, but nothing flowed into her heart. In desperation, she implored in the words of the Sixty-first Psalm; "Hear my cry, O God; attend unto my prayer. From the end of the earth will I cry unto thee, when my heart is overwhelmed lead me to the rock that is higher than I." The words rang, hollow and meaningless, giving her no comfort.

"Oh, Lord, when will this seal be broken that I may pray again? When I need Your comfort the most, it is kept from me. This punishment is nearly as great as losing Esther. Together, it is almost more than I can bear.'' Her words fell flat and wingless against the great tree trunks, then dropped lifeless onto the forest floor.

The men didn't return that night. In the noisy preparations for bedding down those who were keeping Norah company, Mercy, unnoticed, climbed the ladder to the loft and slid into her narrow bunk under the eaves. She lay quite still as the conversation ceased and sleep settled over the cabin. Only occasional coughs and little cries disturbed the otherwise heavy stillness of the night. Then she, too, slipped off into a troubled rest.

Out of the darkness a wide, slobbering mouth came toward her—pointed teeth gleaming white and wicked. As the great mouth opened, she gazed into the cavernous depths and saw Esther crouching inside. Mercy's terrified screams awakened the other sleepers, and Saba shook her until she was thoroughly awake and gasping for breath.

"Thank you, Saba, thank you,'' she whispered and wiped the cold sweat from her brow.

"I'll get you a drink of water.'' The girl disappeared down the ladder into the room below.

Mercy could hear the hum of voices and knew Saba was explaining what had happened. Each night since her rescue, Mercy had had disturbing dreams, causing her to wake trembling, with heart racing. But she had managed to contain the terror and no one had known, until tonight.

She heard Anne's voice. "Apt to keep happening until she gets it worked through. Might even recollect the whole night she was lost.''

Saba handed Mercy a cup and the cooling liquid slid down her parched throat.

"Do you want me to sit with you awhile?'' Saba offered.

While Mercy would have preferred to be alone, she

didn't want to reject the girl's unexpected offer of companionship. "Yes, I'd appreciate that."

Saba lowered herself onto the plank bed, produced a damp rag, and gently wiped Mercy's face. "I remember when you used to do this for me and how good it felt." Laying the cloth aside, she commanded softly, "Roll over."

Mercy did as she was bidden and Saba, with her strong young fingers, kneaded the knots from Mercy's back and neck until she relaxed and grew drowsy. At last, she slept peacefully.

The days and nights passed, endlessly, tension mounting as no word came from the search party. Some of the women drifted back to their homes to tend the livestock and care for other necessary chores, but most of them returned—with food to replenish the Wheelers' dwindling supply and with rekindled interest in the unfolding drama. As the conversation flowed around her, Mercy knew that this story, perhaps embellished by vivid imaginations, would make its way along the river for years to come. And now no one could bear to miss the ending— however tragic it might be!

Each day Mercy escaped the constant cheerless talk as soon as her minor duties would allow. And on those nights when the paralyzing fear released itself in her dreams, providing fodder for the next day's gossip, Saba—blessed, unruffled Saba—was always there to soothe her again to sleep.

At last, late one afternoon just as the sun was casting its dying rays through the thick canopy of trees, the men straggled into the clearing, joyless and defeated. Only scraps of their conversation penetrated Mercy's confused mind.

" . . . tramped the woods from Dan to Beersheba." "Mite couldn't possibly have walked as far as we looked." " . . . raked it with a fine-toothed comb."

Daniel gathered his family, including Mercy, around him. "We found hoofprints and a place where Indians made a fire for the night. Ben's refusing to give up, and he's stayed to follow the tracks." Daniel paused and wiped his eyes. When he continued, his voice, barely a whisper, quavered so that he could scarcely be heard. "I think she's gone, Norah." Daniel shook his head, and his shoulder heaved with sobs. "Just vanished."

Silently the neighbors packed up and left, respecting the family's need to grieve, unobserved.

In the following days, Daniel and Phelan busied themselves with hunting and fishing to restock their larder. Mercy and Saba tended the garden and gathered wild berries. Only this time, they ventured no farther than shouting distance of the cabin and sounded the horn frequently to reassure Norah that all was well.

At last, Ben, too, gave up and returned. He'd followed the tracks of the horseback Indians until they separated deep in the forest where the tracks grew so faint he could no longer see them.

That evening, the Franklin family dropped by and brought with them Anne's sister who'd just arrived from Philadelphia for a visit. Much to Mercy's dismay, the girl had lost no time in learning of Ben's marital status and spent the evening flirting with him in a practiced manner. While Ben didn't encourage her, neither did he overtly discourage her advances.

While the others relaxed after supper, seeking some relief from the heat of the early summer evening, Mercy slipped unnoticed into the woods.

As she walked through the forest the trees began to take on a life of their own. Some, who spent a great deal of time in the woods, said the trees had hearts soft as humans. They told how the pole of the cross of Christ's crucifixion had been cut from pine wood and that was why the pine tree always bled. The cross-piece, they claimed, was carved from a quaking ash; ash has trembled ever since and can never live longer than the thirty-three years of our Lord.

When Mercy was little, she'd learned a song about the birds and beasts covering lost children with leaves until they could be found. But Esther *hadn't* been found, and a beast had caused all this heartache in the first place.

She turned her steps slowly back toward the cabin as dusk deepened the green shadows. She thought she heard voices, sounds of children playing, and she stopped quickly to listen, but it was only the click of beetles in the air or of water gurgling over logs and rocks.

Following the sound of the water, she wandered toward the river. Again she heard voices, but this time it was not her imagination. The soft rumble of Ben's rich bass counterpointed a light soprano. Mercy stood motionless, hidden by the trees. There, on the riverbank, unaware of her presence, Ben and the vital young woman sat facing each other. Her laugh drifted easy and free over the water and blended with the river sounds.

Still as a doe, Mercy watched as the girl reached up and took out the combs in her hair, letting blond curls tumble free over her shoulders.

Mercy's hand stole to the side of her face hidden behind the cap ruffle. The tears rolled unnoticed, dampening the front of her bodice as, silently, she crept through the dark woods, back to the cabin.

CHAPTER 10

MERCY SLEPT LITTLE and, at the first hint of light, she dressed and descended the ladder. The house kept its sturdy silence even as she tiptoed through the front door and stepped into the mist-dimmed morning. Wrapped tight in her cloak, Mercy stopped to watch a doe and her fawn grazing serenely at the edge of the woods.

The doe, muscles taut, raised her head and sniffed the air while the fawn stiffened and held a statue-like pose. Detecting danger, mother and babe, with long graceful leaps, disappeared into the shrouded woods. Mercy continued to keep her vigil, waiting and listening as she had each morning. At last, she heard a dry branch snap, the creak of leather, its scent carried on the light breeze fragrant with wildflowers.

Then she recognized Constant's soft nicker and the reply of the pack horse. Ben! The brief jangle of halter rings, followed by the soft plop of horses' hooves, told Mercy Ben was leaving. Apparently he had said his goodbyes last night after she had stolen up the ladder to nurse her aching misery.

She listened until the sounds of Ben's departure mingled with those of the awakening forest, and she could no longer distinguish one from the other.

She breathed a deep quivering sigh. Ben's silent leavetaking made this day's beginning even more sad and difficult. Worse, she knew she would feel the same sense of desertion each day hence. Perhaps time would ease the edges of grief. But in the meantime, she had to live with the knowledge that the two people she loved most were gone forever. "Oh, dear God, help me," she sobbed into the deep dark void.

Mercy carried the milk bucket to the barn, sagged down on the little stool, and rested her head against Matilda's warm flank. Mechanically, her fingers flew, sending streams of steaming milk into the big bucket. As she felt the cow's stiff hair against the side of her face, Mercy realized the ruffle was not in place. Well—no matter. It was no longer important who saw the scar.

Tears began slowly, just gentle little trickles at first, but soon they were keeping pace with the steady flow of milk in Matilda's pail.

The measured, late-spring days marched irreversibly into summer, but Mercy's grief remained undiminished. Mercy faithfully read her Bible each day and prayed, but no joy filled her, no love sustained her, there was no comfort in the words of beloved verses. Still, she continued the empty ritual.

Her memory of the "terrible night" remained locked within her while the story of the bear with the shredded ear spread up and down the river and grew with each telling. When folks came to visit, they brought tales of hairbreadth escapes and thrilling adventures with the old bear.

Old Flop Ear, as he became known, had been shot at least twenty times at close range, with no ill effects and had broken traps and stolen bait frequently. Even such events as fresh milk curdling within minutes and

105

vinegar refusing to sour were attributed to the sighting of the beast. Some people concluded he was a shrewd old fellow—a rogue bear, sullen, morose—an aging bachelor who lived alone and behaved erratically because he had no wife to keep him in line. Others wanted him slain at any cost. Mercy listened quietly to all the stories, but remembered nothing of her own encounter with him.

Summer ripened into autumn. The days grew shorter and the nights crisper. With the gathering of the garden's bounty, Norah, Saba, and Mercy smoked, dried, and salted, filling the storeroom to overflowing.

But no matter how busy the days, each night Mercy's thoughts turned to Esther. And on the October morn that marked the child's birth, Mercy could scarcely bear to look at the empty place next to Saba. She could almost hear Esther softly crooning her special birthday greeting to herself as she had been doing every birthday since she'd turned two.

Mercy couldn't bring herself to get out of bed. If there'd been any tears left, she would have cried. Instead, she lay dry-eyed, staring at a spider spinning its winter home under the eaves.

"Come on you lazybones! Breakfast's getting cold!" Norah called up the ladder, her cheerful voice slicing through Mercy's sadness like a cleaver. Mercy was appalled by Norah's indifference. How could she so callously dismiss the anniversary of her own child's birth—just seven years ago?

"I shall be down shortly." Mercy fumbled for her clothes. She pulled on warm stockings and topped her brown dress with a wool shawl. Tying on a fresh white apron, she quickly twisted her hair up under the mobcap. Clambering down the ladder, she hurried out to the washstand. The cold water with slivers of ice still floating in it quickly brought her to life as she splashed generous handfuls over her neck and face.

Entering the kitchen, Mercy stifled a gasp when she saw the table set with Norah's loveliest linen and fine china and silver. A celebration—and Esther still gone?

Mercy slid into the empty chair and, out of habit, lowered her head for grace.

"Dear Lord," Daniel prayed, "for what we are about to receive, make us truly grateful. Help us to recognize all Your gifts and accept each one with a loving heart. We will never forget the bright spirit You shared with us for so short a time, but lift from our hearts the grief which has laid so heavy there. Let us welcome with joy the little one coming new from You. Let us love this child with the same devotion we gave our precious Esther. Amen."

"What's Papa saying?" Saba asked.

Daniel reached across the table and clasped Norah's hand. She lifted her glowing face.

"Papa is telling you that the Lord's seen fit to send us a baby, a new little one to love and shelter."

"Mama, that's wonderful! When?" Saba asked excitedly.

"Sometime in late April or early May." Norah squeezed Daniel's hand.

"You need a baby to play with, Ma." Phelan blushed as his voice cracked. Then he admitted, "We all do."

The family looked at Mercy, but she couldn't find her voice. So that explained Norah's laughter of late, and the tender glances she had exchanged with Daniel. Mercy cleared her throat. "I can see how delighted you are—all of you. The babe will find a welcome here."

"But how do you feel, Mercy?" Daniel prodded.

"It doesn't really matter how I feel, does it, Daniel? You and Norah are pleased and so are Saba and Phelan. That's what's important. I'm just the aunt, and I love all my nieces and nephews."

"I've worried so about how you would take this news," Norah said. "I know how much you loved Esther."

"You loved her, too," Mercy countered.

"Yes," Norah said softly and tears rimmed her eyes. However, she blinked them quickly away. Smiling over her family, she said, "And now we'll celebrate the coming of the new little one and the birthday of the one who is no longer with us. 'The Lord giveth and the Lord taketh away.' We shall be grateful this day." She spoke with a resolute strength that defied sorrow.

Mercy ate all she could force past the lump in her throat.

When everyone was finished and empty plates crowded the table, Daniel slid his chair back and Norah watched him carefully. He cleared his throat and toyed with a spoon. Alerted, Mercy wondered what his words would be.

"Our grain is ready to take to the mill in Brookville. I figure we can be loaded and ready to travel by noon. With the new one coming, Norah needs to make some purchases so she can start sewing the infant's clothes."

"You remember, Mercy, I gave away everything when we left Virginia," Norah said.

Mercy nodded and smiled.

"We also need to buy our supplies for the winter," Daniel continued. "Can't count on good weather much longer. Phelan is old enough to stay and care for the place. Can you be ready by noon, Mercy?"

Mercy watched the boy's face fall. He was of an age to want to see the sights. "If Phelan doesn't mind going, I'd really prefer staying here," she said.

"I don't think it's a good idea for you to be here alone." Daniel's face was grave.

"You're only going to be away three, maybe four days. If I have any problems, I can always call on

Anne.'' Turning to Phelan, she asked, "Will it upset you too much to leave?''

He was grinning from ear to ear. "I'll force myself.''

"Then it's settled,'' Mercy said firmly.

Daniel continued to protest, but the last thing Mercy wanted to do just now was to go out in public. Besides, her brother needed to be with his family on occasion, without a chaperone, and so she remained adamant in her determination to stay behind.

With much bustling, the family got off shortly after noon, and Mercy gave thanks for the solitude. Looking about for something to occupy her time, she saw the baskets Norah had set out in readiness for a nut gathering trip. Mercy remembered the directions Anne had given for finding the best trees. After seeing to the cow and its calf, she prepared a lunch so she could stay out longer and make the trip worthwhile.

But there was a moment of apprehension before Mercy stepped out the cabin door. This would be the first time she'd ventured any distance into the woods since that fateful day last spring.

The gray-green shadows that brooded over the forest then were no longer in evidence.

In October, the woods stood subdued as the earth changed to the palette of autumn colors. Mercy watched the birds, millions of them it seemed, feathered nations with languages and dialects, preparing to migrate. Their songs filled the air and rose as praise to the Almighty One.

The simple grandeur lifted her thoughts Godward. Then in one brief instant, all sound ceased and a deep peace welled up in Mercy's heart and spread, warm and glowing, throughout her body. In this moment, Mercy knew that wherever Esther was, she was safe and secure. She slipped to her knees and clasped her hands in grateful prayer.

"Thank you, Lord, for such a welcome gift. Thank

you for letting me come back to You and again feel Your blessed presence. My cup truly runneth over."

She had no idea how long she knelt while her starved soul renewed itself. At last, she took a deep breath and felt a wide happy smile spread over her face. It seemed an eternity since even the briefest of smiles had crinkled her eyes and dimpled her cheeks. She bounded to her feet with an energy she hadn't felt in months, grabbed up the basket, and singing at the top of her lungs, marched off in search of ripened nut trees.

The crags above the valley lay deep in indigo shadows, their harsh tree-less lines softened by the crisp air of the early autumn morning. Behind, the sky flamed with the deep red-orange streaks of sunrise. Upon an outermost crag, a bear stood, dark as the rock itself. He flicked a shredded limp ear and sniffed the misty smoke-fouled air rising from the low-lying river plain. This was no ordinary bear. He was wild and terrible, powerful and rangy, with green luminous eyes glittering in the first rays of the sun.

He swung his huge, dish-shaped head on a heavy neck, thick with muscles and deep fur. Then reaching for a scent, he thrust his snout up again into the slowly warming air. These last few autumns he'd been late in hibernating. For all his plundering and devouring, the comfortable, lazy autumnal heaviness of his younger days came slower every year. This made him short-tempered, volatile, dangerous.

He remained standing for a long time, silhouetted pitch-black against the sky now lightening to pale orange and morning. His head etched sharply on the horizon, his powerful neck stretched at a slant from the enormous mound of muscle between his shoulders. Here lay the source of the great swiping power that fed him—made him the most awesome carnivore in the forest.

With no warning, he thundered a roar of possession and waited while it echoed over the valley. Satisfied his declaration had been heard by any trespassers, he reared upon his hind legs, five hundred pounds of wild force towering against the sky. Jaws agape, on wide flat feet he spun a slow deceptively gentle dance. Then, as suddenly, he snarled at the new sun, bolted down the mountain, and disappeared into the trees.

Mercy crossed the bridge and set off on a path leading into the woods. Along the route she found all manner of nuts—hickory, beech, hazel, and walnuts. She started to gather, then realized she passed this way on her return home and could quickly fill her one basket. Another day soon, she would return with Saba and they could fill several baskets for storage over the winter.

Since all was well at home, Mercy decided to do some exploring. Her heart felt so light, her feet fairly flew along the unexplored paths. Time sped as quickly as she and soon it was mid-afternoon. She found a glade in which the sun still shone and a spring, sparkling clear, bubbled from the earth. Here, she made herself comfortable on a log and ate her lunch. Food and warm sunshine coupled with her lack of sleep last night made her drowsy. She stretched along the log and slept.

The sun moved behind the tall trees until they shaded the glen. With only her shawl for warmth, Mercy grew chilly and awakened, aware that she must find the trail and quickly retrace her steps to the nut trees, or she would be returning home in the dark.

Though she walked swiftly, her progress in the race against descending night was too slow. She looked up to see tall dark crags looming above the trees, their rugged outline crouching stark and forbidding against the sky. The sun dropped behind their peaks, seeking sanctuary for the night, leaving Mercy to face the darkening wilderness.

Suddenly a deep growl rose from the ground almost at her feet Startled, she sprang backwards. The basket sailed forward, striking an enormous bear standing in the middle of the trail where a moment before there had been nothing. Old Flop Ear!

He glowered at her through wicked green eyes and shook his mammoth head so that the shredded ear flapped, limp and ragged. Blood from a recent kill coated his front paws and throat. He pulled his mouth into a snarl, permitting bloody slaver to ooze from between the deadly sharp teeth and dribble over his chin.

A glacial chill descended over Mercy as she recognized Old Flop Ear and stared trance-like at the ugly creature.

Old Flop Ear growled again, nuzzled the offending basket, then with one bat of his mighty paw, sent the container flying into the brambles where it hung, swinging crazily. This seemed to amuse the creature. He rocked his huge black body back and forth, imitating the motion of the basket. This unexpected and incongruous act served to restore Mercy's dazed senses. Picking up her skirts to allow more freedom of movement, she raced head-long into the forest. Anticipating death, Mercy prayed fervently and sincerely that God would receive her and forgive her many sins.

Another furious growl very close-by echoed through the forest, and the noise behind her grew louder and nearer. Mercy, her breath coming in great painful gasps, tried desperately to urge her aching legs forward.

She cast a furtive glance over her shoulder—a second bear had joined the first. Disoriented by the added menace, she lost what little ability she had left to concentrate and tripped over a large tree root.

Quickly she scrambled to her knees in time to see Flop Ear step on a loose rock and lose his balance.

The next instant the other bear was upon him, seizing him by the nape of the neck and sprawling halfway across his back. Surprised and caught off balance, Flop Ear went down. The other grizzly sank his teeth into the base of Flop Ear's neck. Flop Ear snapped his jaws furiously and came up choking on a mouthful of dirt and debris.

Infuriated, Flop Ear gave a sudden twist, flipped upside down, and dislodged his antagonist. They lay a short distance apart, their sides heaving. While they caught their breath, they rumbled back and forth at each other. Since Flop Ear had apparently forgotten about her, Mercy dared not move lest she jog his memory. She lay, statue-like, scarcely breathing. The two opponents rested for such a long time Mercy had about decided they were going to call their battle a draw. Then a small nut-colored bear sauntered out of the woods and sat down to watch.

Here was the signal the great grizzlies needed. They went at each other again, wrestling end over end, flattening bushes and tearing up the forest floor. Round and round Mercy the two giants fought their deadly duel. Old Flop Ear went down. An explosive grunt punctuated the air as his opponent leaped on top. They rolled over and around each other, slashing with bared claws, coming dangerously close to Mercy, threatening to smother her with their combined weight. She tensed her body and waited, eyes closed. Nothing happened! She looked up to see them wrestle apart and stand, blowing and pawing the ground, as though they were performing a ritual dance around and over her fallen body.

She held her breath against the inevitable moment when they discovered her presence and turned from each other to wreak their anger on her. Too fearful to watch more, she averted her head and arched her body to receive the blows that must soon rain down.

Then a bright light exploded in Mercy's brain, and

she saw Esther standing in front of the big hollow tree, frozen by fear as the huge black bear stalked toward her. The events of that terrible night began returning to Mercy with unnerving vividness.

A monumental thud next to her shook the ground and her eyes flew open. A huge creature was down, only inches away. Grunting and crashing, one of them charged off through the thicket. The forest reverberated with the roar of Old Flop Ear as he heaved himself to his feet and pounded after the intruder. The smaller bear gave a disgusted grunt and also disappeared into the woods as quietly as she had come.

Mercy remained motionless until she could no longer hear the sounds of battle, then offered a prayer of thanks for her life. Her legs, weak and trembling, refused to hold her, and so she sat until her fright subsided.

At last when she was able, she rose, brushed herself off, and with shaking hands, set her clothing straight. Looking about, Mercy found she had run so deep into the forest she couldn't see the rugged skyline. Nothing looked familiar. She was lost! At the spot where she stood, she dropped to her knees and prayed, not to be saved, but for courage to endure whatever was in store. And then she gave thanks for the gift of prayer which had been restored to her.

CHAPTER 11

MERCY KNEW THAT ONLY WITH GOD'S HELP could she survive the October night alone and unprotected in the forest. That first awful time with Esther, the weather had been warm and even though it rained, she had had her cape. This time of year ice formed in the water bucket at night; the temperature was already dropping and she was wearing only a light shawl. She must find some sort of shelter, a cave or a hollow tree, and quickly while there was still enough light to find her way. *Please, dear Lord, direct my feet to a safe place*, she prayed. To give herself courage as she set forth through the unknown woods, she began repeating the Twenty-third Psalm.

What had been a friendly forest in the sunlight became, with the closing in of night, a hostile wilderness. Tiny hairs on the back of her neck prickled at strange rustlings in the underbrush and threatening snarls issuing forth out of shadows high in the vine-entwined trees. She gave thanks for the crunch of the newly fallen leaves under her feet which brought memories of happy fall days when she was a child. Mercy concentrated on these times as she felt branches twist about her ankles and try to trip her. Bats darted at her, narrowly missing her face and head. She tried hard to remember they were only feeding and wouldn't hurt her, but all the same she kept biting back the urge to scream.

Mercy had had little experience in the wild out-of-doors, preferring to stay by the fire and listen to tales told by more adventurous souls. *Yea, though I walk through the valley of the shadow of death, I will fear no evil: for thou art with me; thy rod and thy staff they comfort me,* she quoted.

By keeping these comforting words before her, she managed to fight down the panic threatening to engulf her. She knew that her unreasoning terror had been at least partially to blame for Esther's loss. She must not allow that to happen again. By concentrating on the Scripture verses, she would be reminded that God would protect her. Rising on shaky legs, she set off. When she crossed a well-defined path she gave thanks and instinctively turned left, hurrying along the trail as though she knew where it led.

The path was too well-used to be merely an animal trail, and this sign brought hope. *He leadeth me in the paths of righteousness for his name's sake.* With a new serenity, she concentrated on finding shelter for the night. And she began keeping a sharp lookout for a hollow tree or cave. However, there was none to be found. Perhaps it was just as well. The memory of the huge bear rising out of a hollow tree and stalking Esther made that shelter less and less desirable the longer she searched.

She was intent on finding a cave when, suddenly, she stopped short. Did she smell fresh wood smoke? Could there possibly be a cabin nearby? Her heart leaped at the thought and hope became stronger. She quickened her steps in the direction of the scent, noting that it grew stronger by the minute.

A small clearing appeared and there, in the middle, stood a newly built cabin. A thin trail of smoke issued from the cat-and-clay chimney.

"Thank you, Lord. You have truly directed my feet." She instinctively clasped the ruffle of her cap to the side of her face and hastened around to the front of the cabin. The sturdy slab door stood open and a small fire burned on the hearth, but nobody appeared to be about.

"Halloo," she called bravely. There was no answer. She cleared her throat and tried again. "Anybody home?"

Still, there was no answer. "That's strange," she murmured. "People familiar with the woods don't leave cabin doors open, especially at dusk." Even Mercy knew that small creatures—mice, chipmunks, squirrels—sought refuge for the night and could do a great deal of damage once they got inside. Whoever lived here must be a recent comer to the wilderness. Standing in the doorway, she surveyed the room. Nobody was here.

She must look outside for the owner and quickly, for it would soon be totally dark. A fenced area a short distance from the house indicated animals needing protection. She hurried to look inside, thinking the cabin occupant might be feeding his stock. Opening the leather-hinged gate, she peered in. There under a rude shelter stood Constant, the pack horse, and a heifer contentedly munching their evening ration of grain.

Ben! Mercy trembled at the knowledge, that she had stumbled upon his cabin, and forbidden memories and feelings washed over her. Emotionally battered and exhausted, she leaned against the stable wall, letting the memory of their last night together by the river surface in her mind. She pictured his face with its luxurious beard and warm kind eyes, felt his lips, warm and caring, on hers—his arms holding her safe and secure. Then the other scene with Ben and Anne's niece broke its bonds and poured out. She shivered at that remembrance and fervently wished she had found some refuge other than Ben Tasker's cabin!

She stared at the animals, who gave her only cursory glances between bites. She wished they could tell her where he was. Deep within, a feeling of uneasiness began to stir.

"Ben," she called, looking carefully about the fenced area. He had obviously been here recently to tend his animals. But where was he now? She latched the gate behind her and turned, letting her eyes sweep slowly over the clearing.

"Ben!" she called a bit louder, but there was still no reply to her summons. Where was he? Dusk faded quickly now. A moonless sky would provide no light.

Forgetting about covering her face, she gathered her skirts and with increasing apprehension ran about the clearing, shouting his name. She made a full circle and came to lean, breathless, against the stable gate. Only silence greeted her.

The pricks of fear grew, becoming more intense by the moment. Something was terribly wrong. "Please, Lord, help me find Ben," she prayed aloud as she searched for any trace of him. However, if anything was amiss, she didn't recognize it. It was as though he'd simply walked out the cabin door and vanished.

Frightened now, she walked aimlessly until weariness forced her to stop. Leaning against a tree at the edge of the glade, she fought the tears which spilled over her cheeks. Impatiently she wiped them away with the back of her hand and prayed again for courage and God's guidance.

A brief gust of wind brought a whiff of smoke, and she remembered the small fire with its back log nearly burned away. Striking a flint to start a fire was no easy matter, she knew. She must not let it go out! By now, the little remaining wood would be nearly consumed. Hurrying into the cabin, she added more logs from the nearby stack and waited to be sure they caught.

With the fire burning vigorously, she hurried back outside. *Dear Lord, where is Ben?* He had to be closeby. Was he hurt? What on earth would she do if he were injured and lying out in the forest somewhere? *Mercy, move! There's no time to stand here worrying!* If he were wounded or ill, he would surely die or be killed in the night if he wasn't found and cared for.

Returning to the cabin, she located some torches Ben had prepared for such a time. Thanking God Ben believed in being equipped for emergencies, she quickly thrust a torch into the fireplace and watched it flame into light.

The flickering shaft, nearly as tall as she, cast strange and deceptive shadows over the clearing as she walked into the woods. Using the cabin as the center, she began making ever widening circles through the woods, constantly calling Ben's name as she walked. The snarling growls and whines of animals she disturbed kept her in a continual state of alarm. Again, she repeated the section of the Twenty-third Psalm that had subdued her fright earlier.

The torch light flickered and cast such strange shadows, it was hard to distinguish the real from the imaginary. As she tried to step softly so she could hear any moans or cries for help, her foot caught on something heavy concealed in the grass, and she nearly tripped. Lowering the light, she felt through the leaves on the ground until she touched a cold metal object. She held it to the light. The long thin barrel, etched a dull brown to prevent rusting and protected by a thin film of oil, showed loving care. Bringing the stock closer into the light of the torch, she recognized the smooth burnished walnut carved with a coat of arms. Ben's rifle!

He kept the weapon at hand at all times, an extension of his arm. He must be in serious trouble! Who or *what* had knocked it from his grasp? And where was he now?

She sniffed the barrel. Although she knew little about guns, she could tell this one had been fired recently from the acrid smell of gunpowder.

She couldn't leave the gun here to rust in the night dew, but it was too heavy for her to carry, along with the torch. Besides, she neither knew how to load nor fire it. Leaning the rifle against a river birch, she left it to mark the tree near the place where she had found it.

Despair swept over her like a thick penetrating fog. Tiny as she was, what could she possibly do to defend herself against something big enough to frighten Ben so that he would abandon his rifle? Cold tremors of fear rippled through her. She fought down the nearly overwhelming urge to bolt to the cabin where the firelight glowed through the single window, giving an aura of peace and safety.

"Mercy," she admonished herself. "You're the only hope he has. Stop thinking of yourself and get on with finding him."

She took a few tentative steps and stopped again. The shadows created by the torch leaped through the forest like grotesque dancers, darting and weaving through the bushes and lower tree branches. Two round phosphorescent pinpoints glimmered just beyond the circle of light, then narrowed threateningly. A long, low snarl made her blood chill. The bears! Her hands shook so, she nearly dropped the light. *All wild things are afraid of fire,* she remembered through her panic. Praying earnestly for help, she thrust the torch in the direction of the menacing growl. The glinting slits vanished as silently as they had appeared. *Thank you, God, for your protection.*

The palms of her hands grew slick with perspiration

and she could feel beads of sweat run between her breasts and down her back, moistening her chemise and the bodice of her dress. The night air sapped the warmth from the damp clothes, leaving her clammy cold. She started to shiver and, even though she clenched her jaws tightly together, her teeth chattered.

"B . . . B . . . Ben," she called in a quavering voice.

The forest took her call but did not return it, and though she listened intently, she heard only the rustle of dead leaves still clinging to the trees and the faint rush through the evergreens as a night breeze pushed through the woods.

He had to be here. He *had* to be! He would not have gone about unarmed, particularly at night.

She checked again to be sure she could still see the glow of firelight through the cabin window. Having moved only a few steps away, she grasped the torch with both hands and lowered it so she might more thoroughly examine the ground. Stepping carefully so as not to damage or destroy any signs, she bent to search under the bushes and low-branched evergreens.

At last her search was rewarded. Close by a stand of berry bushes, the light showed a patch of grass, matted and scarred. Reaching down to lift the lower branches, she grasped something moist and sticky clinging to the leaves. A shudder ran through her body, and she jerked her hand away. When she examined her palm by torchlight, she saw that it was streaked with fresh blood. Frantic, she looked about. "Ben! Ben, answer me!"

Then she remembered the bear, its fur stained with fresh blood. "Oh, dear God, no!" she cried. "Ben!"

Forcing herself to take several deep breaths, she calmed down enough to think. The blood had been low on the bush, so she dropped to her hands and knees to look into the thicket, being careful to keep the torch away from the branches. She could see nothing. The underbrush, protected from the killing frost, was still in full leaf and reflected the light rather than allowing it to penetrate. Scrambling to her feet, she searched for a way around the brambles. Using the old birch and the cabin as markers, she made a wide circle until she was on the other side of the shrubs. With one torch held low, she walked cautiously through the tall grass, stopping after each step to examine the area around her before moving further.

A gust of cold wind caught the torch, and the flame veered away and sent off a trail of black smoke. Mercy shivered and wished she had thought to grab a cloak from the cabin. Another step. The light advancing before her revealed matted grass glistening with fresh spatters of blood. There had been a vicious fight here recently. Although she could hear nothing, she felt Ben's presence somewhere near this spot. Icy fingers of dread gripped her. She knew beyond any doubt that he was terribly hurt, perhaps even dead. And with the knowing, a strange calm descended over her.

She plunged the torch into the dark along the bloody trail. With each step Mercy's heartbeat quickened. Her mouth dried and she tried to lick her parched lips, only to find her tongue cleaving to the roof of her mouth. Slowly, almost afraid of what she would find, she searched the path. Then, the torch light picked up a moccasin-clad foot.

Her involuntary scream rent the night. "Oh, Ben!" Mercy stared, barely comprehending. *He's dead!* The thought jolted her shocked mind, and her head began to spin. Her knees started to buckle and she quickly drove the torch against the ground to prop herself up. As she stood, transfixed by the sight at her feet, rage filled her. Esther—and now Ben! All that she held most dear had been destroyed by that demon. She thrust the torch to the sky and cried, "I will rid this earth of you! I will! Even if it means my own life!"

Trembling from the emotional explosion, she turned back and knelt beside Ben's body. He lay face down, one knee bent and a hand outstretched, gripping a clump of young bushes. She looked at his blood-smeared back and felt the loneliness of his death penetrate her heart. Her eyesight blurred through the rising tears, and she crumpled against a log.

Then, an almost inaudible moan reached her ears. She crawled to Ben's side and leaned close. There was another weak moan. He wasn't dead! Not yet! He had simply collapsed in the attempt to crawl to safety.

Propping the torch against a log to light the area, Mercy took the outstretched wrist and tested for a pulse. She could find none. Mustering all her strength, she rolled his limp body over and gasped! His torso, head, and arms, were covered with blood—his face, unrecognizable from deep claw marks. A feeling of total helplessness swept over her. She had no idea how to deal with such severe injuries. Never in her life had she been called on to do more than bandage a cut finger or kiss a bump better. It was Norah who prepared and administered the medicine, set broken bones, sewed up cuts. Now here Mercy was, faced with wounds that would challenge a battlefield surgeon.

She stared at Ben, paralyzed by the magnitude of his injuries. Another moan. She wiped away the tears and squared her shoulders. "Mercy," she said quietly but firmly, "God directed you here and if you'll listen to Him, you'll know what to do." The impact of her words gave her confidence. Never before had anyone depended solely on her for anything. Even that night in the forest with Esther, others had been searching, too.

Though she knew she had to stop the bleeding, Mercy stood for a moment, horrified by the sight of his blood pooling on the ground. It was accumulating at a frightening rate where he lay. Forcing herself from the trance, she left the torch, pushed her way through the wall of bushes, and raced toward the cabin.

Once inside, she searched until she found scissors and one of the sheets Norah had sent with Ben as a housewarming gift. A full bucket of water stood on the wash bench. Lighting another torch, and carrying the water, she hurried back to Ben as quickly as her burdens allowed.

In her haste, water splashed down her dress and into her shoes, but she was much too occupied to notice the discomfort. Positioning the fresh torch opposite the first one to counteract the shadows flickering over Ben's inert body, she began tearing the sheet into strips, then cut away the shredded buckskin jacket and washed the blood and debris.

At last, his wounds lay clean and exposed. His left arm and hand were twisted in unnatural angles, but she must stop the bleeding of the deep gouges down the left side of his face, shoulder, and chest before she could attempt to set the bones. Watching his chest intently, she detected a slightly irregular rising and falling. He was still alive. Praise God!

She knelt, absorbed in working over the raw wounds and staunching the blood that was still flowing freely. Nothing seemed to be helping. Ben was going to bleed to death even as she worked so desperately to save him. *God, You've got to help me. Show me what to do.*

Most of the water was gone, so she grabbed the bucket and dashed to the small stream not far away. When she returned, all the wounds had stopped bleeding except for two deep gashes on his shoulder and chest. These still showed little sign of slowing.

If she could get the slashes packed and wrapped tightly, perhaps the bleeding would stop. Her glance fell on moss growing on nearby trees. She ripped it off, filled sheet strips with it, and packed the wounds. Tearing more of the sheet into strips, she wrapped the cuts. Only his nose and mouth showed when the bandaging was done.

She had to set his arm before those gashes could be bandaged. Clenching her jaw to keep from screaming, Mercy probed blindly into one of the deeper cuts, and found the bones snapped in a clean break. If only there were someone to pull on the arm while she guided the bones together. *Help me, Lord. Guide me and give me strength.*

She steeled herself against the sight, pulling and twisting with a strength she had never possessed. At last she felt the bones slide into place. Ben made no sound through it all.

Quivering and drenched in perspiration, Mercy sank onto the ground. With his face bandaged, she couldn't monitor Ben's reaction, but shallow rising and falling of his upper chest assured her that he had survived thus far.

A moment's rest and then she was up, sponging away fresh blood from his mangled arm. She must find something to brace the forearm. Beyond the flickering light, she spied some dead branches close to the spot where Ben lay. Choosing the best, she trussed up his arm. The effort was far from adequate, but it would do for tonight. In the morning, she could make some liniment and re-wrap all his wounds.

Ben's weight and size made it impossible for her to wrap the gouges on his shoulder and chest, so she laid a covering of sheeting over the wounds as some protection. She sat back on her heels, exhausted, but the temperature had dropped and Ben must be covered. Unable to move him into the shelter of the cabin, she was forced to leave him once again. This time she returned to the cabin for another torch and quilts.

Before she covered him, she scraped away the blood-stained leaves and grass from around his body, then replaced them with fresh ones. Spreading the quilts over him, she arranged the burning torches, and crawled under the bedding next to him, trembling with cold and exhaustion. The dampness from her dress and shoes seeped into her bones, and she grew more miserable with the passing moments.

At length she realized that she must find some other way to warm them both. Wearily, she arose and began gathering dried grass, sticks, and branches with which to build a fire. After layering them as she had seen others do, she set a torch to the dried grass. The leaping flames ignited the smaller branches and twigs, then the larger pieces of wood, and soon she had a roaring fire. She felt the chill begin to leave her as the air about them heated. When the fire blazed vigorously enough, she rolled up a large piece of log. This banked the fire for the night and served better than torches to keep the wild animals away. She could extinguish the precious torches and conserve them for another day.

She stood by the fire until she was warm, then crawled back under the quilts and curled herself about Ben, but his deathly cold skin took her warmth and left her chilled. She slid out and stood by the fire again and again, returning to share the heat with Ben, but he was scarcely less cold than before. Staring into the fire, Mercy again pleaded, "Please be with me, Lord." And then she remembered Norah's wonderful stones, heated at the edge of the fire, and wrapped in flannel to warm cold feet.

She lugged stones from the stream bank and placed them around the fire, losing track of time as she waited for them to heat through. At last they were ready. Wrapping the rocks in towels and flannel from the cabin, Mercy placed them around Ben's body. Then she crawled in beside him. With the quilts tucked over the rocks to trap the heat, they were soon warmed.

"Thank you, Lord, for being at my side. I know you have gone before me to save Ben. Please remain to guard us both through the night." She sighed, laid a hand on Ben's shoulder, and slept.

CHAPTER 12

AT DAYBREAK MERCY AWOKE. She lay for a moment, letting the sleep slide away, feeling Ben's body next to hers. Though he had remained unconscious throughout the night, Mercy now knew the comfort of a man's solid bulk so near. She rose reluctantly. The separation was real, knife-like, and Mercy knew she was ready to fight with everything within her to make her life into more than the shadow it had been.

Gently, she laid back the quilt and ran her hand over Ben's skin. His temperature felt normal to the touch. Carefully covering him, she watched his breathing. Although still shallow, it had grown regular in the night. How long would he lie there, stuporous? He must soon eat and drink if he were to regain strength and to fight the infection that was sure to come.

Dreading to leave him long, Mercy knew she must gather more wood and secure supplies from the cabin. First, however, she set a pot of water to boil over the coals. There was liniment to make and bandages to be soaked. Bless Norah for all the things she had sent with Ben, including some medicinal herbs!

Mercy picked her way through the frosted clearing to the cabin. She did hope she could locate the directions Norah had had her write concerning the blending of certain herbs for special treatments. Mercy hadn't bothered to learn the more complex mixtures, believing she would never be called upon to prepare any but the most simple of them.

A loud bawling from the stockade reminded her that the cow needed milking. At least, here was something she could do well. Inside the cabin, she refueled the fire, grateful for an abundant supply of wood. Then, locating a milk bucket, she hurried out to the palisade.

She found a familiar little three-legged stool and began this day as she had most of the days of her life—her head buried in the flanks of a cow, draining its udder into a bucket.

After finishing this chore, she released the animals from the shelter to graze inside the fenced acres. Later in the day, if Ben was doing well, she would come back and stake them out in the clearing where the grass still grew lush and tall.

Carrying the full bucket of milk to the cabin, she covered it with cheesecloth and went in search of Ben's springhouse. There was a well-worn path leading to the sturdy wooden structure at the edge of the stream. Inside, on shelves above the water, were yesterday's milk covered with a thick coat of heavy yellow cream, freshly roasted meat, and a rich yellow round of butter. This reminded her how hungry she was, and she brought everything back to the cabin.

Inside, she found several loaves of bread, wrapped and stored in a wooden box. She prepared a hearty breakfast, then searched out the herbs together with the instructions for their use. Finding the recipes for Norah's liniment and one to ease pain, she selected the necessary ingredients. Taking the bottle of liniment already prepared, she loaded her arms with the utensils, food and supplies, and hurried back to Ben.

He still lay as she had left him. "Ben," she called softly. "Ben, can you hear me?" With his face obscured by bandages, it was hard to tell if he gave any response. She was wasting precious time. Besides, since she had to unbind all the cuts and wash them, it was well if he remained in this unfeeling condition.

She set a mixture of powdered golden seal and myrrh to steep, then ate her breakfast.

Tearing the rest of the sheet into strips for clean bandages, she gently removed the blood-soaked dressings. In the daylight, the gashes looked even worse. Some, particularly those on his shoulder and arm were still oozing blood. It sickened her to see in the full light the vicious raking his body had taken. The cuts on his face ran into his beard, and she needed to shave him if they were to be treated and heal properly. Did he have a razor? She would look later.

With the herbs steeped, she used the warm solution to soak the wounds clean. Since his arm had not only been clawed but bitten, the danger of infection was greatest there. She soaked the large gaping wounds in the solution, hot as her hand could bear.

Ben groaned, long and thin and raspy. Though grateful for the sound, it tore at her heart. She gritted her teeth and forced herself to continue digging out the debris he'd driven into the wounds as he crawled. Swallowing the gorge rising in her throat, she worked to cleanse the deep ragged gashes.

Tears formed and spilled over onto her cheeks while she bathed the gouges. Not knowing if he were still conscious, she whispered, "I'm nearly done, Ben. Only a bit more."

His good hand groped for her arm and tugged weakly. His lips moved soundlessly. She couldn't hear what he said, but she felt he knew who she was and understood she was trying to help him. After the effort, he drifted down again into blessed oblivion.

She left the entire arm soaking in a solution of hot golden seal and myrrh. Norah's directions said to keep the wounds soaking until they closed.

Now she was ready to shave him, an act she had only watched her father and Daniel perform. Putting more water on to heat, she went to the cabin in search of barbering supplies. To her surprise she found an old shaving mug, brush, and razor. She tested the blade with her thumb as she had seen Daniel do. It felt very dull even to her inexperienced touch. In the absence of a razor strop, she took a whetstone, together with the rest of the things, back to the little glen.

As she knelt by his side and spread clean towels under his chin, his lips moved. Still, she could not understand his words. Frustrated, she looked into his face. "I don't know what it is you're trying to say, Ben. Say it one more time, and I'll concentrate."

Then she read once more the words he uttered soundlessly. "Mercy, don't leave."

"No, Ben, I won't leave, not as long as you want me to stay." Whether he spoke from longing or merely from pain, it was enough to know that he needed her now.

Trying not to let him sense her uncertainty, Mercy said firmly, "I must shave your beard in order to treat you properly. I hope the razor's sharpened well."

She took scissors and cut the long dark beard and hair as short as practical. Then she lathered his face with soap from the mug. He lay absolutely still as she poised the blade above his cheek and began scraping carefully. The right side wasn't too difficult, but she grew tense as she set about trying to remove the whiskers near the angry gouges. Though his eyes were closed, he winced as she made the first pass around a gash. It wasn't worth inflicting more pain on him, she decided, and left the rest of the beard as she had clipped it with the scissors.

Clean-shaven, his neck appeared to be nearly the size of a young tree trunk, large powerful muscles running to his shoulders. The deep claw marks stood out distinctly. They had narrowly missed ripping the blood veins, thus sparing his life. "Thank you, dear Lord," she whispered as she stared at the miracle before her. She thoroughly cleansed these wounds and bound them as best she could.

With a wooden mallet, she pounded the meat, added salt and herbs to the water in the kettle, and set it to steep. She must have something nourishing for Ben to drink when he awoke.

While the stew simmered, she searched for a way to erect some sort of covering. The mist and dew last night had dampened the quilts and there was no shade from the sun during the middle of the day. Remembering the rude half-faced camp, she set about finding poles that could be rested on the log not far from where Ben lay. The woods were full of brushy twigs that hadn't yet lost their leaves, so she soon had constructed a rude shelter. It would do just fine if it didn't rain.

The little clearing was pleasantly warm in the afternoon sun and a soft breeze blew, keeping the mosquitoes away. Satisfied with her work, she sat and leaned against the log to rest and watch the soft white clouds passing overhead. She must have dozed, but when she heard a soft cough from the woods, she sat straight up.

There he was, his ugly head with its deformed ear, swinging slowly from side to side, his silver-tipped black coat glistening in the sun. She stared into his eyes and felt she was seeing into the very pit of hell. She wanted desperately to look away, but she remembered hearing Ben tell Daniel that once eye contact was made with a wild animal, it should never be broken, for they considered the act a sign of submission and would attack for the kill. Praying for strength to hold on, she returned glare for glare. She had no idea how long she fought the visual battle. It seemed hours had slipped by when she felt Ben stir and moan. *Oh Ben, don't move now, please. Dear Lord, quiet him. If Flop Ear recognizes him, we both may be dead.*

In answer to her prayer, Ben grew still while she continued to stare into the evil eyes. Then unexpectedly, Flop Ear growled a harsh warning and broke the gaze. He turned his attention to the animals grazing innocently in the clearing. Mercy felt her mouth go dry. Then, before she could move, the brutish beast turned and plowed his way through the underbrush and was gone.

With thoughts of the bear keeping Mercy in a state of continual apprehension, the evening chores seemed to take forever. What if Flop Ear returned to find Ben helpless? Tomorrow, if he were strong enough, she must have Ben teach her to load and shoot his rifle.

She slept outside the small shelter this night so she could be nearer and tend the fire. Besides, now that Ben was occasionally conscious, she didn't want him to wake and find her curled next to him. The declaration of love she'd made to him at the river still rang in her ears and colored all her actions. She wondered if he had thought about it since.

The accumulated smoke and haze of the autumn day blew away and the night sky, brilliantly clear, covered them. There was no moon, but in the starlight she could see the highest crag where the old bear reigned. It towered, ragged and dark, against the purple sky. Mercy stared into the fire and gave thanks for her blessings this day. Ben's wounds were healing nicely and his strength was slowly returning. He showed no sign of fever and although he wasn't fully conscious, there were lucid moments, promising the return of full awareness. She should have been able to rest, but something made her vaguely uneasy.

Suddenly she knew what it was—there was no sound! A healthy forest was usually alive with a cacophony of sounds—by day, the chirping and croaking of woodland birds and animals; by night, the haunting hoot of an owl or the howling of wolves. Tonight, except for the murmur of the stream, silence hung eerie and heavy. She desperately wanted to ask Ben for the meaning, but he was too far gone from the effects of the catnip tea she had prepared to aid in a restful sleep. She listened while his breathing grew even deeper and more regular.

Mercy tried to tell herself that the ominous feeling was probably her overactive imagination, and she snuggled down against the warm rocks, under her quilt. Still, she couldn't shake the apprehension and stayed alert for a long time. Finally, weariness overcame her fear, and she slept.

The sound of cracking branches woke Mercy as some heavy-footed animal came up from the river and stood just beyond the range of the firelight. She could make out a large dense black shadow, but not clearly enough to be sure what it was. She had the impression of solid bulk, but her sleep-sodden mind seemed reluctant to identify the animal. She stiffened! A bear! Flop Ear? She lay rigid, scarcely daring to breathe, praying the creature would go away. With every muscle and nerve tensed, and eyes straining, she watched until the shadow melted away. Off in the pines a twig snapped, and something rustled through the newly-fallen leaves. Then, the silence remained absolute. Only Ben's deep breathing sounded over the gentle babbling of the stream. Just when Mercy thought she must scream from anxiety, the crickets began their tenuous intermittent chirpings. Gradually, others joined the chorus until their din filled the whole forest. Thus reassured, Mercy fell into the deep sleep exhaustion brings.

The morning of the second day brought another round of responsibilities. It was afternoon before she finished with the animals. There was so much milk now, she simply poured it on the ground, after which, she staked the two horses and the cow out in the clearing to enjoy the sun and the fresh grass. Then, she spent a great deal of time soaking Ben's wounds thoroughly, applying liniment and making his broth. He drank hungrily.

"When do I get some solid food?" he asked through clenched jaws.

"When you can open your mouth to chew. You took an awful blow to your jaw as you know."

He lay back, drained from the effort of swallowing the broth. "Can't believe I'm so weak."

"You lost a great deal of blood. Rest now. I'm going to the river to wash the bandages."

Although he didn't speak, a look of fright flashed across his face—something Mercy had never expected to see there. Always, she had relied on the menfolk, depended upon their strength and skill. First, Pa; then, Daniel; more recently, Ben. Hadn't he blazed their trail, felled woodland creatures for their food, cared for them all? It unsettled Mercy, weak and vulnerable as she was, to realize he was now depending on her. *Lord, only by Your help can I carry this burden. It is Your strength that must see us both through.*

Finally Ben slept soundly, and Mercy felt it was safe to leave him for a short time. She arrived at the stream with the basket of laundry. Gathering her skirts to kneel at the water's edge, she looked across the river to the bluffs, then froze, staring with trance-like fascination at the gigantic bear. The wind riffled the long silver-tipped black hair along his back and shoulders. She could see the broad skull with the fur furrowed between his brows. One ear drooped, disfigured and useless. Flop Ear! She wanted to run, to hide from the killer, but she feared she might wake him and bring him down to the helpless Ben.

The bear twitched his snout, protesting the flies buzzing about his head. One forepaw was casually draped over the other, and his barrel-like sides rose and fell in the slow rhythm of deep sleep. She lost track of time as she stood rooted in her tracks. Finally, Flop Ear leisurely lifted his head and began slowly swinging his muzzle back and forth, sampling the air. Then slowly he stood, stretched, rose up on his hind feet to get a better view. On the low cliff overlooking the river, he towered like a mighty black marble statue against the crisp blue sky.

Peering directly at her, it seemed as if he were taunting her. "I don't want you yet. You're not frightened enough. I want you cowering and quivering before me, begging for your life and that of your man. Then I shall enjoy disposing of both of you."

Mercy didn't move. For one moment more he stood there, then dropped onto all fours, leaving nothing but empty sky. He lumbered into one of the runs the bears had tunneled through the entangled brush of the thicket. Wedging his massive body deeper and deeper into the underbrush, brutishly strong shoulders forced their own tunnel beneath the low limbs, and the tunnel closed behind him.

Mercy's knees gave way, and she sank onto the soft sand. It seemed Flop Ear was toying with Ben and her—hovering close, sensing his power over them, smelling her fear—until he became bored. Then, with two or three swipes, he would kill them both and curl contentedly into his winter den secure in the knowledge that he had eliminated the intruders in his woods.

Mercy forgot about the washing and hurried back to Ben. He must tell her how to load and fire his gun. She had sworn to kill Flop Ear and kill him she would. She must!

Stepping softly lest Ben still slept, she knelt outside the shelter and looked in on him. He had thrown back the cover and lay bare to the waist. Muscles rippled over the deep golden tan of his good right arm and shoulder. His chest was broad and covered with dark curly hair. Ben was marvelously built, and regal, rather the way she pictured King David. A joy surged up in Mercy.

His face was terribly pale, though, and she felt a tenderness that rivaled the joy. She would not tell him about Flop Ear. Later—when he was stronger.

"Ben, how are you feeling?" she asked softly.

"My head—it pains me some."

"Drink some more broth. That should help."

She held his head so he could sip from the cup. It pleased her that he drank such quantities of the rich broth. He would regain his strength quickly if no infection developed. He slept again briefly.

"Mercy," he called, his voice distant and quivering.

"Yes, Ben." She hurried to his side.

"More broth? My head . . . "

"Right here." She let him drink all he would. Then he slept again. As quickly as possible, she tended the animals, then set the rocks to heat. There was very little sleep this night, for Ben's pain grew worse until the broth gave no relief at all. An occasional low moan escaped, and each time Mercy flew to his side.

Early in the morning of the third day, he seemed to be worsening. "Oh, Ben, I don't know what to do for you," Mercy cried softly.

"Nothing to do. Just bear it . . . Can't get any worse." He spoke through parched lips that no amount of water seemed to moisten.

Even in the pale light Ben's face looked gray and drawn. Only a faint tic in his right eyelid betrayed his suffering. Inwardly she wept for him.

"Tell me where it hurts," she said.

"Shooting pain along both sides of my head," he whispered. He turned to face her and a puzzled look spread over his face. "What's in the air? I don't smell smoke."

"Why?" she asked.

"You look kinda dim-like." He rubbed his eyes and opened them again, then shook his head slightly. "Still hazy." He turned to look full at the sun. "Is the sun shining?"

It was a bright autumn day. The air, crystalline. Not wanting to alarm Ben, Mercy busied herself. Soaking a towel in cold water, she laid it over his eyes.

The cold compresses did their work and Mercy watched the tension drain away as Ben slept once more.

When he woke, it was afternoon and the sun was streaming into the tiny glade. "Mercy?" His voice sounded stronger.

"Right here, Ben." She crawled under the shelter and knelt beside him.

"I didn't mean to sleep away the day. What time is it?"

"You're much better at this than I, but judging from the sun, I'd guess about three o'clock. How close did I come?" she asked, thinking he was testing her ability to tell time without her timepiece.

"I . . . I . . . I don't know," he stammered, his voice thinned to a whisper. He moved a trembling hand in front of his eyes. "Mercy?"

Her heart plunged. What was the matter with him? "Ben, I'm here. Right beside you," she answered in a tight strained voice.

He fumbled until he found her hand, then clutched it, and she felt the panic radiate from him.

"I . . . can't . . . see." Each word was an icy chip of despair.

Mercy moved to cradle his head in her lap. She tried to deny the unthinkable. Taking a deep breath, she stiffened her spine. He must not suspect how frightened she was.

"Look at the sun," she ordered.

Ben turned his head toward the warmth, but there was no recognition in his eyes. The silence seemed to last an eternity before Ben gave a long shuddering sigh. "I'm blind, Mercy. . . . Blind."

"You must rest now. What has happened is only temporary." Mercy's words were filled with hope, but her voice was hollow.

Ben lay back on the pallet of quilts she had made for him and seemed to escape into a world of his own. Shut off from him, Mercy eased herself up where she could use the back log of the shelter for support. She sat quietly, watching him blink his eyes again and again, trying to raise the curtain of blackness. He touched them with the fingertips of his right hand.

She didn't know what to say to bring him comfort, so silence crowded in again.

At last, he said in a voice, hushed and trembling, "The pain's gone. Gone away and left me blind."

Mercy slid down beside him. "My momma once told of a man brought home from the woods, blinded by a terrible crack on the head when Indians attacked his camp. Lay most of the week without sight. Then one day it came back good as new."

Ben lay very quiet for a long time before he said, "Would to God that might happen to me."

Little beads of sweat stood out on his forehead. His breathing grew rapid and shallow—the pattern of fright. She felt his skin. It was damp and clammy. Quickly, she spread a quilt over him and lay next to him, holding tightly to his hand.

Mercy didn't know how long they lay like this, but the sun had shifted until it no longer shone into the glen. Ben finally said, "It's as if I've been put inside a cave with no light at the entrance."

"You've been badly hurt, and healing takes time.

As your body heals, so will the injury to your eyes. You'll see again." This time her voice carried the conviction of faith.

"You really believe that, don't you?"

"The Lord has asked very little of me but faith. When I give Him that, He takes care of me."

"Then, how do you explain Esther?"

"I can't, Ben. But I do know that the Lord loves her, and that He is caring for her wherever she is. That reassurance came to me as real as the conversation you and I are having. I am absolutely sure of His power and goodness."

Ben shook his head.

"It can't hurt to have faith, Ben. You can't see now when you have no faith. Perhaps believing will help restore your sight. Please promise me you'll try."

He took her hand and squeezed it.

"Good! The Lord *will* heal you. I know He will!" Mercy's voice rang firm and sure, a testament to her faith. "Now it's time to feed you and your animals and prepare for the night. Will you be all right if I leave for a little, to milk the cow?"

"Is there a sizeable fire?"

"Yes, but I'll add more logs just for good measure."

He sought and found her hand. "Hurry back," he pleaded.

Mercy's heart swelled inside near to bursting. *Thank you, Lord, for letting me know this feeling once in my life.* No matter what happened, she would always have the memory.

CHAPTER 13

ON THE FOURTH DAY. heavy clouds hung low in the sky holding the air close around them, moist and cool. When Mercy awoke, she prayed, *Oh, dear Lord, please don't let it rain. Ben isn't strong enough to walk to the cabin, and I can't carry him.*

She turned so she could look into the shelter. Ben lay on his side, his face relaxed and peaceful. He slept a deep natural sleep, a healing sleep, a sleep that would restore his sight.

Ben stirred, slowly opened his eyes, and blinked. He rolled onto his back, rubbed his eyes, and blinked again.

Using his uninjured right hand, he touched the bandages on his face, felt the missing beard and ran the tips of his fingers over the bare face. Moving on, he investigated the splinted and bandaged arm and gently touched the uncovered gashes on his shoulder and chest. They were scabbing over well, even though they were deep and serious.

Not wanting to startle him, she watched in silence. His hand groped over the still-warm rocks, touched the dirt, stopped a second, then rustled through the dry leaves. Puzzlement spread over his face. His lips framed her name.

"I'm here, Ben," Mercy said softly.

He licked his dry lips and attempted to clear his throat. "I dreamed you had gone away and I was left alone. It was so real I still feel shaken," he said, his voice a heavy hoarse croak, very unlike his usual resonant bass.

Mercy threw back her quilt, pushed her hair from her eyes, and reached for the cup to take him a drink of water. He tried to sit up when he heard her.

"Please, don't do that. You'll split those gashes open again and you can't afford to lose more blood." She hurried to his side, and gently pushed him down. "Let me hold your head up so you can drink." She cradled his head with her arm as he lifted himself slightly to bear some of his weight on the uninjured arm. With her hand on the smooth warm skin of his bare shoulder, she reveled in the weight of his body against her. All the time she'd tended him when he was unconscious, her thoughts had been directed to saving his life. Now that he was conscious, she sensed a new intimacy and, with a slightly unsteady hand, she held the cup to his lips while he drank greedily. "More?"

He nodded and she refilled the cup. Again he emptied it. "Enough?"

"Yes. Thanks." His voice sounded clearer and even a bit stronger. Lying back, he sighed, slowly and shudderingly. " I keep feeling gentle hands ministering to my wounds, a soft voice comforting me. It is so far-fetched that you should be here. I constantly fret that I'm still delirious. When I wake I'm afraid I'll learn you're a mirage." His hand fumbled until he found hers, then he closed it inside his large, warm palm. "Tell me now, how you came to be in my woods."

Praying that he would believe her, she told her story.

"Thank God you managed to escape that old rogue," he said. Bringing her fingertips to his lips, he kissed them gently. "You're an answer to prayer. You know that, don't you?"

Her heart quickened and she had to fight to steady her voice. "I don't believe I do."

"The last thing I remember after the bear mauled me and before I passed out was praying for mercy. God, in His wisdom, sent me you. Now I know it was you I was praying for all the time."

She wanted to throw herself into his arms and tell him how she loved him, believed what he said came from his love of her. Instead, she reminded herself that Ben's love for Genny was too strong still to think of another. He needed Mercy; but he didn't now, nor would he in the future, ever love her. She must continually bear that in mind and not delude herself a second time.

Managing a cool tone, she said, "I'm flattered, Ben, truly I am, but I can't imagine anyone in your desperate circumstances praying for me to come—helpless as I am. Were I in your condition, I'd be screaming to high heaven for Norah!"

"Norah's knowledge is impressive, I agree, and she's extremely efficient, but your gentle fumblings are a greater comfort."

Mercy wanted to ask him how he knew, but she bit her tongue and kept quiet. "Your wounds must be less painful this morning."

"Yes. Guess I'm getting used to it. The scratches only pain me when I move." He glanced, sightless, in her direction. "The worst part is waking to find it's still dark."

"Your wounds can scarcely be called 'scratches.' Old Flop Ear vented his fury on you." Mercy cast about for something comforting to say. "As for the blindness, it's likely only temporary, but until you regain your sight, I suppose you'd best let me help you."

"You're right, I suppose. Can't remember when I felt so useless." He clung to her hand as a child would cling to its mother. "At first, it seemed I was dreaming you were tending me. I thought I was dying and you were here, helping me on my way to heaven. Then later, when I felt your gentle hands and I hurt too badly to be dead, I was afraid my yearning for you to be here had made you real. That really frightened me."

Ugly spears of suspicion stabbed Mercy's heart. Was he being nice to her, saying these things so she wouldn't leave him? She could never desert him under these circumstances, no matter what he said.

"Mercy?" His voice betrayed his feeling of help-lessness and his fear of abandonment.

"Don't fret, Ben. I shan't be far away unless I tell you." Confusion boiled through her. Her strong invincible hero lay, a pleading frightened little boy, depending on her for everything. Had he any idea how slim were their chances for survival? Could Mercy, protected, sheltered, even pampered, be expected to provide for another more helpless than she?

"Mercy?" he called timidly.

"Yes, Ben."

He licked his lips and cleared his throat. She could picture him digging his toe in the dirt in his embarrass-ment. "Nothing," he finally said.

What was it he needed? And then it dawned on her. She could feel the heat rise, flushing her face and neck.

Reaching for a pan, she handed it to him. "Here's a bread tin. I'm going to the stream to bathe."

She was thankful he couldn't see her scarlet face as she quickly gathered a towel and soap and hurried along the trail she'd created with her comings and goings to the river. Stripping from clothes she'd slept in for days, she held her breath and plunged into the cold water. Once past the initial shock, the water was refreshing and invigorating. After scrubbing herself thoroughly, she wrapped in the towel, washed her clothes, and hung them over the bushes to dry.

"I'm going to the cabin, and then I'll tend your animals," she announced as she passed by Ben.

Inside the cabin, she restoked the fire. Then, without conscience, she rummaged through Ben's clothing until she found a faded red shirt made of linsey-woolsey. *Genny probably grew the flax, sheared the sheep, gathered the dye, spun the thread, and loomed it into material before she sewed the shirt*, Mercy thought grudgingly. She slipped the garment over her head and watched the tail puddle around her feet and the collar slip down over her shoulders. It swallowed her!

Diving back into the box, she found a delicately carved ivory brooch. She used this to pin the slit in the front. A piece of rope lying carelessly in the corner served as a belt. Making deep rolls in the full gathered sleeves until her hands stuck through she stood at last, decently covered. She did hope her clothes dried soon, though. The bulk of the ill-fitting garment hampered her movements, turning even routine tasks like gathering wood for the fire into clumsy undertakings.

It wasn't until she sat with her head against the cow's flanks, watching the streams of milk foaming in the bucket that she thought of Daniel and the family. Strange how she could have put them so completely out of her mind for four days. She was so aghast at her thoughtlessness she stopped her milking. If they had returned from Brookville yesterday, they would be frantic with worry by now. If they hadn't returned until today, there would soon be a search party combing the woods, looking for her as they had for

Esther. If Norah lost the baby on her account, Mercy would never forgive herself.

The cow bellowed unhappily. "Yes, yes. I'll get on with the job," Mercy said, and took up her task. All the while, though, her mind was racing. She couldn't have left Ben unconscious and alone, not with Flop Ear keeping a tireless watch. At last she concluded she had done the only thing possible. If she made him a crutch, perhaps Ben would be strong enough by late afternoon to make it to the cabin. Once inside, he would be safe. Then she would rush back to the settlement to let the family know she was alive and well, get some food and supplies, and return. Blind and helpless, Ben could not be left alone. Everyone would surely understand.

This morning Mercy took time to make sure each teat was thoroughly stripped of its milk. She'd dashed through the milking the other days, but Ben seemed so much better today she felt she could take a few extra minutes. Ben depended so heavily on this little heifer, it wouldn't do to have her going dry in the middle of the winter.

After depositing the fresh milk in the springhouse, Mercy scooped some heavy cream from yesterday's milking into a small pitcher. She knew of a small grove of wild peach and plum trees nearby. The fruit with fresh cream should make a fine treat for breakfast. Gathering the last of the roast and another loaf of bread, she hurried back to the campfire.

"Seems you've been gone a long time," he said. "Probably just as well, though. Has given me some time to think."

"I've been rushing with the milking, so I took a little more time to do it right." She kept her voice brisk, giving no hint of the emotions roiling just beneath the surface every time she looked at him. "I'm going now to gather some fruit for breakfast. I hope you're hungry."

"Starved. How many days since I've eaten?"

"Last night."

"Why don't I remember?"

"Possibly because you were only partially conscious, and I made you broth which you drank."

"From the meat in the springhouse?"

"Yes."

"I sighted a big elk the other day. Roasted some and smoked the rest."

"A good thing you did, too. Having the makings for broth probably helped save your life. Do you need anything more before I leave?"

"No. But don't be gone long." An edge of fear textured his voice, and Mercy thought again of a little boy afraid of the dark.

"The trees are very close. You'll be able to hear me if you listen."

She purposely scuffed through the leaves and stepped on dry branches to leave a trail of familiar sounds. While she picked from the heavily laden trees, she hummed a favorite tune of Esther's. If she were in Ben's place, she would find it very frightening to be left alone. This was a strange thought for her to entertain after she had sought solitude for so long. Not in fourteen years had she been so continuously in the presence of another person. And she didn't even have her face covered. There seemed no need when he couldn't see, and it gave her a sense of freedom she had long ago forgotten.

Suddenly she wanted to hear his voice. "Ben, can you hear me?"

"So clearly I can almost see what you're doing."

"I'm hurrying. I've just noticed a persimmon tree. Do you like persimmons?"

"I do. With the early frost, they should be just right."

"Then I'll pick a few and be right there."

The trees grew from the middle of a bramble of

raspberry bushes, and Mercy struggled to find a way to reach the fruit without ruining Ben's shirt on the barbs. Finally she succeeded in getting close enough. Raising her arm, she clasped her hand around a large ripe persimmon. Before she could pluck it from the tree, however, a bear on the other side of the bushes rose up on its haunches before her. He gave forth a groan that chilled Mercy's soul and left her without voice. She began trembling in every limb, her hand still clutching the fruit. For the life of her she couldn't move. With a deep fearsome growl, it started through the underbrush toward her.

"Mercy!" Ben shouted.

She looked to see him struggling to sit up. The sight jolted her into action.

"Don't you dare move from there!" she screamed at him. Jerking her hand down and finding the large fruit there, she hurled it at the advancing bear. The ripe persimmon smashed over the bear's face. He stuck out its tongue, liking what he tasted, and reared up on his haunches again. Finding the tree, he began rapidly consuming all the fruit he could reach.

Mercy took advantage of the temporary distraction to move cautiously out of sight and back to Ben. "Shhh," she whispered as she knelt beside the trembling, sweat-covered man. "It's all right. I threw a persimmon in his face and he's busy stuffing himself."

"Is it Flop Ear?"

"No. Looks like a young one to me. Just trying to top off its weight before it goes to sleep for the winter." Mercy was astounded at her own words! Was this nonchalant woman the same person who'd been so terrified a few minutes earlier?

"Have you any idea where my rifle is?" Ben asked.

"Yes. I found it in the grass and took it into the cabin out of the damp. Would you like me to fetch it after we've eaten?"

"Yes, and my powder horn and gear box. I'd feel better if the necessities and the rifle were close-by."

She waited by his side until the bear ambled off into the woods, then she set about preparing breakfast.

When they were finished eating, she set the box and the gun beside him. He ran his fingers over the weapon and fumbled about in the supply box. Giving the stock a slap, he swore under his breath and thrust the gun at her.

"Don't know why I thought I could clean and load her," he said bitterly.

"If you'll tell me how, I can do it," she offered.

"You're going to have to do more than that, I'm afraid."

"What do you mean?"

"I don't want to alarm you, but I don't think Old Flop Ear has forgotten me. He's been stalking my cabin for weeks and now that he knows I'm hurt, he'll be back to finish the job. Can't imagine why he hasn't been back before now."

The resolute strength that normally underlaid Ben's manner had returned, but Mercy kept to herself the fact that Flop Ear had been back already, at least once.

"You're going to have to *shoot* the gun as well," Ben was saying.

"*Shoot* it! Ben, I can barely *lift* it! I've never had anything to do with a gun in my life!" Mercy looked at the rifle she clutched awkwardly. How on earth did he think she could hold it and shoot it when it was as long as she was tall?

"You mean to tell me you didn't at least load guns during the Indian raids?" He sounded unbelieving.

She knew what he was thinking. Every woman on the frontier knew how to load and fire a gun, for she must fight for survival right alongside her man. "I was so little, they always sent me to tend the children. I never learned how," she said timidly. She didn't add

149

that, with one hand holding her cap against the side of her face, she couldn't be of much help.

"Well, today you'll learn." There was a timber in his voice which told her he would brook no nonsense. Both their lives could very well depend upon her performance in the next few hours.

CHAPTER 14

BY THE TIME SHE HAD CLEANED and loaded the gun a sufficient number of times to satisfy Ben that she was catching on, Mercy ached miserably. Even though she rested the rifle on a log and held the stock snugly against her shoulder, it was impossible to cushion the impact when the weapon was discharged. When Ben at last called a halt to the practice session, her shoulder felt as if it had been beaten with a mallet.

"I'll feel a bit safer if you clean and load the rifle once more," Ben reconsidered.

Tears of frustration rolled down Mercy's cheeks. "Ben, I can't!" She struggled to keep the sobs from her voice. "I know you couldn't see, but every time I fired, the shock threw me on the ground. If my shoulder isn't broken now, it will be if I have to shoot one more time!"

"Why didn't you tell me?" Ben barked. "Come here and let me feel. Your shoulder could well be broken, though I lightened the powder charge . . . I forget you're no bigger than a minute."

Swiping furiously at her wet face and grateful he

couldn't see her, smudged and sweaty, Mercy knelt and took his hand. Directing his fingers to the bruised area, she sat quietly while he searched uncertainly along her shoulder and upper arm, then retraced his path to her neck.

His hand stopped short, and he fingered the fabric. "What's this?"

"When I bathed this morning, I washed my own clothes and hung them on the willows near the river. I found this shirt in your pack box."

His fingers skimmed again until they encountered the brooch at her neckline. "And where did you get *that?*" he asked curtly. His hand, fisted now, gathered the material in a stranglehold.

Mercy gulped. "The shirt was too big for me, so I had to use the brooch to pin the opening closed. Forgive me. I should have asked."

He released her, giving her a little shove. "Yes, you should have asked. Genny made that shirt—it's the last of the things she made for me." He paused for such a long time that Mercy wondered if he were dismissing her. Then, fascinated, she watched a tear trickle down his cheek. "I carved the brooch for her from whale bone." Ben turned his head away and stared, silent and unseeing, into the forest. Mercy waited until at length she felt he'd forgotten her presence.

Her muscles cramped, and she moved to change position. This act brought his attention back to the little glade. "Sorry," was all he said. He offered no explanation concerning what he'd been thinking. "Take off the pin so I can pull the shirt away and feel your shoulder bones."

With tremulous hands, Mercy unfastened the brooch. When she removed it, the shirt fell open, exposing her bare shoulder and threatening to drop lower. She grabbed the front and held it together, affording her some semblance of decency. She raised his hand again and placed it on her right shoulder which was rapidly turning ugly shades of black and blue.

"Ummmm," she moaned between clenched teeth.

He ignored the pain he was causing and continued to probe along her collarbone and around the shoulder. "Can't feel anything wrong with the bones, but judging from the amount of heat, you do have a bad bruise. You'll need to put cold compresses on it right away."

Mercy repinned the shirt. "I'm going to the river for my clothes and to wash off the smell of the powder."

"Before you leave, would you load the gun and lay it by me? Even though I can't see, I could shoot at the sound if I have to."

Obediently, she went through the steps of loading the rifle and propped it next to Ben. "I won't be long," she assured him.

"Keep a sharp lookout. Bears are restless this time of year."

"You can be sure I will!" she said over her shoulder as she hurried away.

After putting on her own clothes, she returned to the cabin where she fueled the fire and replaced the brooch in the pack box. She'd washed the shirt and as soon as it dried, she would put it away, too.

She was starving from her morning's work. "Hungry?" she called to Ben when she returned to the little glade.

He nodded, but warned, "If you don't put the cold compresses on that shoulder, you'll suffer."

"As soon as you're fed."

"Stop treating me like a baby," he snapped. "I may be blind, but I'm not crippled!"

Startled by his reaction, she bit back a comment. "Very well, if you insist." She spread a quilt over the log to protect his bare back from the rough bark.

By the time he had positioned himself against the log, he was panting with exertion, and beads of sweat stood out on his forehead and upper lip. He gave a sheepish grin. "Guess I should have listened to you. I'm a lot weaker than I thought."

He allowed her to feed him the elkmeat stew, sopping up the juices with hunks of cornpone, but she did not embarrass him by commenting further. Ben Tasker was a proud man.

The sun, breaking through thinning clouds, warmed the afternoon air. With Ben resting, Mercy took time to apply the cold compresses to her shoulder. From the swelling and discoloration, it looked as if she were too late to do much good. All the same, the cold took the heat from the fevered skin and lessened the pain. Wringing out a final compress, she spread it on her shoulder and lay down on her quilt. Both she and Ben slept, waking only when the trees shaded the clearing.

Quickly, Mercy added some big logs to the fire and built it up large enough to combat the penetrating wind.

"How's the shoulder?" Ben asked.

"Better, I think. The compresses and the nap helped. How are you feeling?" she asked as she knelt to look at his wounds.

"Much better, thanks to your expert care."

"It's time to treat those gashes with liniment again. They've been neglected today and that won't do." The firmness in her voice surprised her. It was a good imitation of Norah—so good that Mercy was convinced she knew what she was doing, and she dripped the herbal liniment onto the bandages with renewed confidence.

Upon completing the task, she announced, "I'm going down to the river. With today's sun, it should be dry," she said.

"Where's my rifle?" he asked, his hand groping about.

She propped it against the log and placed his hand on the stock.

"Be sure to call out when you come back."

Even though the fire was burning well, Mercy added a few more logs for good measure and ran down the trail. She hadn't worked so hard in her life, or eaten so much, or felt so alive!

Testing the thick collar, she found the shirt dry and ready to store again. The cold water hadn't rid it completely of the acrid smell of gunpowder, but judging from Ben's concern, she thought it best to store the precious object as quickly as possible. Perhaps another time, when she had hot water, he'd allow her to wash it properly.

She was standing in front of a dense stand of willows and carefully folding the shirt when a bone-chilling roar came from the riverbank. Mercy recognized the deep growl a second before Old Flop Ear broke through the willows, downstream from her. Instantly she knew this was to be the final showdown. Raising his shovel-like muzzle, he tested the air with his blunt snout, then turned toward her in a ponderous, rolling motion, perfectly coordinated. Now he was facing her. His deep black hump and tremendous silver-tinged shoulders glowed menacingly in the late afternoon sunlight.

When he opened his huge blood-red mouth, fanged teeth gleamed white and dangerous. Mercy stood, paralyzed with fear. He paused, a growl rumbling deep inside his chest, and the two of them stood, eyeing each other. After what seemed an eternity, Flop Ear raised on his hind legs, bellowed a fearsome roar, and started toward her again. He swiped the air with a huge paw, the razor sharp claws distended and lethal.

This act shocked her into action and she fled up the trail. "Ben!" she screamed. "It's Flop Ear!" The bear was on her heels, and she expected any moment to feel a blow from the brute's paw.

She raced to Ben's side and grabbed the gun. Turning around, she saw that the old rogue had stopped at the edge of the glade. He swayed slowly from side to side, and growled in a voice like distant thunder. Why had he stopped? Of course! The fire.

"Mercy?" Ben whispered.

"Right here," she said softly as she crawled over the log and pulled the gun across to her. "Flop Ear's on the other side of the clearing. He's afraid of the fire."

"That won't stop him for long. Not in broad daylight. He's just sizing up the situation. You're going to have to shoot him." Ben paused and turned sightless eyes on her. "You know that, don't you?" he asked in a gentle whisper.

"Yes." A chill settled into the marrow of her bones.

Almost as if she were in a trance, Mercy knelt behind the log, feeling the blood pound in her temples, aware of a strange emotion. She and the immense animal on the other side of the glen were united by a singular bond—the resolve to kill.

She wasn't even aware of the tension as her hands gripped the rifle stock. Across the way, Flop Ear stood motionless, smelling the familiar odors of Mercy and Ben carried to him on the wind. Then his glittering green eyes rested on Mercy's motionless figure. The two gazed at each other, issuing a calm challenge. It would be a death duel, with only one survivor.

Slowly, very slowly, Mercy pulled the rifle into position on the log. She looked over at Ben who had rolled onto his side facing her, his blind eyes open and straining. He licked dry lips and wiped his sweaty forehead, pushing unruly strands of damp black hair back with trembling fingers.

Apparently sensing her need to have him talk her through the steps practiced earlier, he said softly,

156

"Hold the stock tight against your shoulder. Sight down the barrel at his head." Ben's voice was surprisingly firm and calm.

Shrugging aside the pain in her shoulder, Mercy raised the gun until she could see the ragged, deformed ear over the end of the barrel. She inhaled sharply.

Ben's hand clenched, and he leaned closer. "What's the matter?"

"He just stood up on his hind feet," she wailed. "And he's coming this way!" Her heart pulsed in her throat, and she gasped for air.

"That's good. Gives you a larger target to aim for. Go for his heart."

Her hands quivering, Mercy readjusted her sights and attempted to steady the gun.

"When you're ready, pull on the trigger slowly. Try not to jerk the gun."

Old Flop Ear continued to advance, one step at a time. Mercy couldn't look and closed her eyes as she squeezed the trigger. Before the first echo, almost with the smoking roar and cascade of fire from the muzzle as the rifle discharged, the bullet entered its target.

Mercy opened her eyes to see Old Flop Ear, looking a bit as though he'd been betrayed, stagger backward with the force of the missile and place his front paws over the wound. Slowly he turned away from the source of his injury and returned all four feet to the ground. He took several steps back toward the woods. Then, as if suddenly comprehending what had happened, the bear whirled about, let go a terrifying bawl and paused to gather himself for a charge.

"Mercy, for God's sake, tell me what's going on!" Ben cried.

She swallowed, trying to find her voice. "He's standing back in the woods, swaying from side to side as though he's going to attack," she said, betraying her panic.

The bear took a faltering step and pitched down onto one shoulder. He offered up a series of earth-shuddering bellows, roaring his anger over his non-functioning legs.

"You've got to reload! One shot won't be enough!" Ben shouted.

As Flop Ear thundered his fury and struggled to rise, Mercy crawled over the log and found the box with the gun supplies. With unsteady hands, she endeavored to get the cap off the powder horn.

"Stay calm," Ben kept saying. "You're doing fine."

"I am not doing fine!" she sobbed. "I can't even get the powder horn open, and I can't remember a thing!" She gave a hard tug and the cap came off. Powder flew out and spilled down the front of her dress. Nearly witless with fright, she stared stupidly at the river of black stain reaching to the ground.

"Mercy, do you need help?" His voice cracked like a whip.

She jerked. "N–no. I don't think so," she stammered when she could speak.

Faltering and uncertain in her haste to perform the still unfamiliar act, tears of frustration and terror rose to dim her sight and complicate her attempt. If she didn't load the gun properly, it would misfire and kill her, or it wouldn't fire at all, and the bear would kill them both. *Lord, help me do as Ben taught me. Please!*

She looked up in time to see the bear shake himself and take a step. "Ben, he's coming this way."

"Hold steady." Ben's words cut across her fear. "Set the rifle butt on the ground with the muzzle pointed away from your body." His deep voice rolled the instructions to her, sure and strong.

"Ben, you can't see what's going on!" she screamed, completely unnerved.

"Mercy, stop it!" he commanded and the power in

his voice shocked her as thoroughly as if he'd taken her by the shoulders and physically shaken her.

She forced herself to breathe deeply and think only of loading the gun. "All right," she said, having regained some control. "I have the muzzle up. Tell me what to do next."

He held up his hand. "Put the bullet in my palm."

She fumbled frantically in his gun box for a little lead ball. Her icy fingers had trouble gripping the ball, but at last she dropped one into his palm.

"Put the funnel in the muzzle for the powder. Take the cover off the powder horn."

His directions were far more detailed than necessary, but the sound of his voice was steadying.

"I'm sorry to do this, but you're going to have to have a bigger powder charge. Pour powder into my hand until it's deep enough to cover the ball."

At that moment she made the mistake of glancing across at the bear. His violent thrashing shook the ground. Trembling uncontrollably, Mercy shook the black grainy powder into Ben's palm until the ball disappeared. She plucked the ball out and dropped it into her apron pocket. Tipping Ben's hand, she filled her palm with the measured powder and dumped it into the small funnel and down into the barrel of the gun.

At a resounding crash, Mercy looked to see Flop Ear lunge to one side knocking a dead tree to the ground and falling heavily beside it. The great bear lay, a dark mound on a bed of yellow aspen leaves, struggling to rise. His cries and grunts were pitiful to hear.

"Tell me what's happening!" Ben demanded.

Mercy pressed her hands over her eyes. "I . . . I . . . I can't look," she sobbed.

"Is he down?" A tinge of panic crept into Ben's voice.

She continued to hide her face.

"Look, Mercy! Look!"

Making a crack between her fingers, she peeked at the huge creature stretched out on the ground. "He's down," she whispered through her sobs, "but he's still moving, trying to get up."

"He's a long way from dead then. Keep loading!" Ben ordered. "Take a patch from the patch box in the gun stock and find the bear grease."

In a terror-induced stupor, Mercy mechanically did as Ben bade her.

"Pour some grease on your fingers and work it into the cloth. When you've finished, lay it over the muzzle."

Mercy looked up and stared, transfixed, as the old bear struggled back onto his feet. She gave a low, tremulous moan. "He's back up and coming this way."

"Don't look at him. Load! Center the patch over the muzzle. Put the ball on it. Be sure the sprue mark's on top."

She fished the lead ball from her pocket and set it on the little round patch of cloth spread over the muzzle. The flat sprue mark left from the fold stared up at her.

"Get the ball started and push it into the bore."

"Ben, you know I'm not strong enough to do that."

He raised up and leaned over the log. "Put my hand over the starter."

She positioned his hand in the air above the short dowel with a drawer knot on the end. She held it steady on the bullet. "Now," she said.

He gave it a smack, and the ball hand patch disappeared into the bore of the gun.

Quickly, she removed the starter and set the ramrod into the muzzle.

"Remember to make the ramming stroke smooth and uninterrupted," he coached. "Look for the mark on the rod, so you'll know when the ball is firmly seated against the powder."

The chill wind increased and blew across Mercy's back, wet with sweat. She shivered, licked her lips, and planted her feet to give her a firm base from which to push the ramrod into the barrel of the gun. Grabbing the long stick, she pushed it even and hard. The rod went in smoother than at any time today. *Thank you, Lord.*

"Got it?"

"Yes. It's in right to the mark." Suddenly, her voice was calm. There was a strength there she'd never heard before.

Ben must have heard it too, for he said simply, "Good girl."

Without further instruction, she placed the hammer at full cock and opened the frizzen. Pouring a small amount of powder, enough to fill the small depression, she closed the frizzen and checked the flint. It was still sharp. She was ready.

Taking a deep breath, she knelt and rested the gun on the log. "Better move back so the sparks don't burn you," she said to Ben.

He slid away, but kept his head turned toward her. "What's the old rogue doing?"

Slowly she raised her eyes. The great black hulk stood on uncertain feet, swayed unsteadily, and took another step toward her. The leaves where he'd lain were stained scarlet and blood trailed as he took yet another step. Deafening roars filled the clearing, making it nearly impossible to hear Ben. "He's coming—one step at a time—directly toward us!" she shouted.

"Aim for his head."

She wiped her palms—one, then the other—on her apron and looked down the barrel until the mutilated ear lined up in the sights. She pulled the stock tight against her shoulder, and winced at the soreness. Carefully, she wrapped her index finger around the trigger. The old bear raised his head and looked her directly in the eye.

Slowly, deliberately, with eyes wide open this time, Mercy squeezed the trigger. Along with the ear-splitting roar, a great puff of acrid smoke and flaming powder shot from the gun. But Mercy didn't see it. The powerful powder charge had sent her spinning backward into the underbrush. She lay, the breath knocked from her, clutching her shoulder. *It's surely broken this time,* she thought.

"Mercy!"

"Here," she called weakly. She opened her eyes to see Ben's head bob up over the log. "Don't move! I'm all right."

When she could breathe normally, she crawled back to the log and forced herself to look into the clearing. The great bear lay still.

"Ben, I think I did it," she whispered.

"Is he dead?"

"He dropped in his tracks. I shot him right in his floppy old ear."

"Then he's dead . . . It's over . . . How are you?"

She reached down and picked up the fallen rifle. "Shaking like a dry leaf."

"Come here." He stretched up his hand and she took it to steady herself as she climbed over the log. "Sit down beside me."

Carefully, she leaned the gun on the log and dropped down next to Ben.

"Let me have your other hand, too."

She placed both frigid hands together in his one large one. He rubbed them vigorously for a few minutes, then asked, "How's the shoulder?"

"Broken, I think."

He probed along the collarbone. "If so, it's not a bad break. Probably be wise to rest it in a sling for a few days though, just to make sure." He smiled at her, a bit crooked and shy. "So you got Old Flop Ear—a tiny mite like you."

"I never could have done it without you, Ben, and

the Lord. You, telling me what to do. Him, giving me the strength." She sighed. "In spite of everything, though, it's sad to see that old bear lying there."

Ben dropped back against the log. "Give me your hands again. They're freezing cold."

He opened his palm and she laid her fists inside. He stroked the backs of them slowly from wrist to knuckles with his thumbs. Her heart beat in strange erratic patterns and swelled inside her breast until it was hard to breathe. An involuntary shiver ran through her like an aftershock, for his ministrations were doing something warm and wonderful to the chill inside her.

Though confused by the intent behind this intimacy, she was powerless to stop him. She let him go on burning a trail across clenched fingers, prying open a fear-locked fist, then slowly turning the palm to his mouth. Mercy watched his eyes close as his lips caressed the inside of her hand. Her fingers curled over his chin, and she shuttered her eyes against anything that might distract her from the magic of his touch. A radiant current bound them together while his kisses lingered across his cupped palm.

Then, with unerring accuracy, he found her lips and they melted together in a rapturous kiss. Mercy lay, captured in his arms, willing the moment to last forever.

"Halloo the cabin!" The shout carried through the warm afternoon air and across the clearing. Ben and Mercy sprang apart and, clutching her arm, she leaped to her feet.

Breathless and flushed, she searched for her cap and nervously swept her hair under it. "Sounds like Daniel," she cried.

Ben raked his fingers through tumbled locks. "I wondered when he'd come for my help in searching for you. Can't understand what in tarnation took him so long. Counted on him, not you, to do away with that bear after I got hurt."

"There's something I haven't told you," she said hesitating. "Daniel and the family were in Brookville. Nobody knew I wasn't at home."

"You have behaved in a very foolish manner, Mercy. What would have happened to you if you hadn't stumbled onto my cabin?" he lectured.

"Halloo," came the call again.

She was reluctant to share this moment with anyone, yet it was inevitable. "Guess I'd better let him know where we are."

She stepped into the clearing in time to greet Daniel and some of the men from the settlement as they came back to the cabin from a fruitless search of the stockade. "Mercy! What in the name of common sense are you doing here?" He stopped in his tracks and his voice was harsh and angry. "Don't you know the whole settlement's been searching for you?"

She hurried to him. "I'm sorry, Daniel. I was afraid of that, but I could do nothing about it."

Daniel interrupted her. "If you planned to come chasing after Ben, you could have told us and saved everyone a great deal of trouble."

"I didn't come chasing after Ben." Mercy was stunned by the accusation. "After you left, I went gathering nuts. A bear attacked me and I got lost."

"The nut trees are *up*river."

He didn't believe her! "Daniel, when one is running for one's life, one doesn't stop and plan a route. Besides, I went down the river in the first place, like Anne said."

"Then, why didn't you fill your basket and come home?"

"You're not listening to me, Daniel. A bear chased me!" Mercy couldn't remember when she'd been so angry. Her own brother accusing her of running after Ben. And he was so furious with her right now, he wouldn't believe anything she said. Better to let him *see* her reason for staying away. "Come with me!"

she snapped, and without waiting to see if Daniel was following her, marched into the woods to where Ben lay.

Daniel stood, assessing Ben's condition. "Doesn't look so bad to me that you couldn't have left him long enough to let us know where you were."

"Daniel!" Mercy was shocked at his callousness. "He's blind—and a bear was trying to kill us both!" She pointed to the great black heap at the far end of the clearing.

Daniel walked down and kicked the old bear in the side, then turned back toward Mercy and Ben. "Great shot for a blind man. You can boast about that for the rest of your life."

"Daniel Wheeler!" Mercy shouted at him. "*I* shot that old bear. *Me!* Poor, helpless Mercy!"

"She did, Daniel, and that's a fact," Ben said quietly. "She's got the bruised shoulder to prove it."

Daniel muttered something and scuffed a bit at the dirt around the bear. "No matter. I still have to take her home. Let the folks know she's not hurt."

Ben struggled to sit up. "If you'd help me get to the cabin before you leave, I can manage fine."

"You cannot manage alone," she said and stooped to give him support as he attempted to stand. "Daniel! You men!" she ordered the men standing near the edge of the glen, looking uncomfortable at having to witness the fight between brother and sister. "Help Ben to the cabin. He's lost a great deal of blood."

Daniel and the other men, startled by the authority in her voice, rushed forward and made a stretcher with the quilts. By the time they carried Ben to the cabin, Mercy had the bed ready, and Ben collapsed onto it like a fallen log. Perspiration ran from him in rivers and his skin tone had turned a sickly gray. Mercy quickly wrapped some warm rocks and nestled them about him, then tucked in the quilts to capture the heat.

"Mercy, go with Daniel!" The strength in Ben's voice shocked her. "I don't need you here. I don't want you here. Now, *go!* "

"Ben, you can't mean that," she gasped, as breathless as if she'd been kicked in the stomach.

"I do mean it. Flop Ear's dead and I have no further need of you. I can manage fine."

Mercy stood staring at Ben, speechless. Not fifteen minutes ago he had been kissing her like she meant everything in the world to him. Now he was sending her away. Was he really so heartless that he could pretend such affection?

"He's comfortable and will be until I get back," Daniel said and grasped Mercy's arm. "You, sister dear, are returning home immediately."

"Daniel, let go my arm. I'm not leaving him until he regains his sight."

Her struggles were in vain, however, for she had no hope of overcoming Daniel's anger. He propelled her along the pathway at a rapid clip, and the men followed at a discreet distance. They covered the miles back to the settlement in record time, where Daniel made short work of explaining the situation, thanked everyone for aiding in the search, and began preparing to return and nurse Ben.

Daniel was still so furious with her that Mercy had the feeling if she'd been a bit younger, he would have spanked her soundly and sent her to bed without supper. No amount of explaining altered his determination that she not return to Ben and only served to increase his anger.

Very well, Daniel Wheeler. You may have your way today, but just you wait. And as for you, Ben Tasker— you've not seen the last of me. You're going to have to look me square in the eye and say what you did today.

CHAPTER 15

It was women like Norah who gave credence to the stories that babies were found under berry bushes. Even in her final weeks of pregnancy, she never looked more than a few well-distributed pounds heavier, and today, the twenty-second of December, was months away from that time. She bustled about, singing her joy at full voice, finishing the last-minute tasks—her secret so thoroughly hidden that not even the most perceptive gossip would guess. The family had chosen not to tell the settlement of the expected baby. Norah said she'd been clucked over enough by the well-intentioned after Esther's disappearance. Now she wanted to be about a normal life.

Even though Brookville was sixty miles away, the Wheelers, along with most of the other families in the settlement, planned to travel there for a Christmas celebration. They looked forward to attending a special church service on Christmas Day and a festive dance the next night. For weeks, the talk among all ages had been of little else.

From the sleeping loft, Mercy could hear Norah

talking to Saba downstairs. "Isn't it a perfect day!" she exclaimed. "I can't get over the families in Brookville opening their homes and inviting us to stay. Think of all the new friends we'll make. I can't remember when I've been more excited."

"Nor I." Saba's voice actually had a lilt to it.

"Do you have some special plans I don't know about?" her mother teased. "Has Anne's boy asked you to the dance?"

"Mama!"

Norah laughed merrily. "Would be nice if he did. Jim's a fine boy. Make you a good husband one day."

Mercy could picture Saba blushing a deep hot pink, secretly enjoying her mother's teasing. Saba had already confided her fondness for Jim to Mercy and his intentions of escorting her to the Christmas dance.

Bells fastened to the harness jangled through the crisp morning air as Daniel and Phelan brought the sleigh up to the front door and began loading the waiting cases.

"If there's nothing more to do, I'm going out and get in the sleigh," Saba said, and Mercy heard the door open and close.

"Hurry, Mercy," Norah called up the loft ladder. "Daniel's nearly finished packing the things. Hand your case down."

Mercy drew a deep breath and prepared to do battle. Since she had said nothing to the contrary, everyone had assumed she was going along. But she was not, and that was that. Daniel still hadn't completely forgiven her for the embarrassment she'd caused in the fall when they'd left her alone and, given even a short time to think about it, he'd carry her aboard the sleigh. That would guarantee the ruination of the trip for all of them. *No, it was better this way. Bitter, but short.*

When she arrived at the foot of the ladder, Norah was buttoning her long fur cape. Daniel, cheeks stung red from the cold and eyes dancing, burst through the door.

"Let's go, ladies." He slapped his gloved hands together as though this act would spur Norah and Mercy to greater activity. "Mercy, where are you cloak and case?" Two giant strides brought him to her side, and he peered intently into her face. "Aren't you feeling well?"

"I feel fine. I'm just not going." She cringed slightly, waiting for the explosion she knew would occur. She wasn't disappointed.

"What!" he roared.

Mercy stood, unmoved. "I'm not going," she repeated. "You need to be a family sometimes, without an old-maid sister tagging along."

"What drivel! Get your things! You can't stay here alone! You proved that when we left you the last time," Daniel shouted, only slightly less forcefully.

"I shall get along very well." Mercy marched to the door and threw it open. "Daniel, you're wasting precious traveling time. I am *not* going."

Daniel faced her with his hands on his hips, his head shaking in his anger. "Planning to run to Ben again?" His words spilled out, sarcastic and bitter.

"After he practically threw me out? Hardly. You heard what he said." Mercy matched him, shout for shout, and Daniel looked confused.

He shook his finger in her face. "Yes, but you still wanted to stay with him. Would have, too, if I hadn't dragged you home."

"You can carry me to the sled and force me to go. That will certainly make for a merry trip and a joyous Christmas." If she could make the idea sound idiotic, perhaps he wouldn't try it.

Shock at her defiance spread over his face and he turned helplessly to Norah. "Can't you persuade her?"

Norah shook her head. "She's your sister. If you

169

can't convince her, I'm sure she won't listen to me." She gathered her fur spread and muff, sailed past Mercy through the open door, and out to the sleigh.

Mercy and Daniel stood fixed, testing each other's wills. He continued his black glare, but she refused to look away. "I swear I don't know what's gotten into you," he finally said. "You've been unreasonable and bull-headed ever since you came back from tending Ben."

"Daniel, come," Norah called. "The children are cold."

His grim look turned to pleading, but Mercy held her ground. She had learned that from Old Flop Ear. "Have a wonderful time," she said, breaking into a delighted smile and following him outside.

He hesitated, then gave a defeated shrug, bent over, and hugged her goodbye. Without further comment he climbed up beside Norah in the sleigh.

Mercy waited on the porch, waving in answer to the chorus of farewells until her family swung into the trees and out of sight. She'd won her freedom at last!

Relieved, she gazed a minute more out over the clearing, sparkling like an iridescent pearl in the morning sun. Great tufts of snow still perched on the tree branches from yesterday's storm, and snow birds twittered busily about their food gathering. Mercy felt a peace born of controlling her own destiny settle over her, and she stepped into the cabin, softly latching the door behind her.

Looking about, she decided that her first chore would be to tidy the rooms. If things were reasonably straight, Norah, who'd always had servants in Virginia, was happy. It didn't bother her that drawers and cupboards might be a shambles or corners filled with dust. She hid what she could behind doors and put furniture in front of the rest. For Mercy, neatness started with the inside and worked its way out.

The next two days were spent happily straightening, scrubbing, and polishing. This was Mercy's Christmas present to the family, for when they returned she would be gone. Daniel was right about her being changed by her experiences with Ben. And because of them, she could no longer stay in Daniel's house, protected but ignored, living her life vicariously.

Christmas Eve stole over the clearing, peaceful and still. A brilliant star shone in the sky overhead and she thought of the Star of Bethlehem. Was this how it was that precious night so long ago? She stood in the gloaming, waiting—tense with listening. All day she had been so filled with thoughts of Ben, she knew he must be coming. She prayed he was. She couldn't bear to think of him spending this special holy season alone.

At last, the cold drove her inside where the water she'd set to heat was boiling. She took the large kettle from the fire and, mixing the boiling water with cold, filled the copper tub she'd placed before the fireplace. Never in her life had she experienced the luxury of bathing in a tub filled to the brim, steaming and fragrant. She had sung all day with the anticipation of it.

After slipping off her clothes, she poured in a few drops of perfumed oil, bought from the peddler man, and tested the water with a big toe. Then breathing deeply of the perfumed steam, she stepped gingerly into the tub and eased down into the oil-slickened water.

When she had soaked to her heart's content and toweled dry, she put on an old robe and emptied the tub. Using fresh water, she washed her hair until it squeaked. After brushing it dry in the heat of the fireplace, she hung up the old robe and put on the baby-blue flannel nightgown and matching robe she'd made with Norah's help. She had embroidered a field of spring flowers over the yoke of both gown and robe

171

and made booties to match. Letting her jet-black hair hang loose, she took her Bible and curled into Daniel's chair in front of the fire. As she waited for Ben, content and deeply happy for the first time in years, she read the story of the Christ child's birth.

The chiming clock on the mantle reminded her of the passing time. When it struck nine times, she accepted the fact that she'd been wrong. Ben wasn't coming, but it didn't matter. Slowly, she closed the Bible and laid it on the table. She added plenty of wood to the fire, wrapped a heated rock in flannel, and climbed the ladder to the sleeping loft. After slipping the stone in to warm the sheets, she pulled the small traveling case from beneath her bed and carefully filled it with her few belongings.

Her prayers said, she slid between the warm covers. Anticipation pricked through her, but she refused troublesome thoughts of the morrow. Instead, she closed her eyes and saw before them the beauty of the star on this most holy of all nights, presiding over the humble stable. She heard the angels announcing the Saviour's birth and watched the shepherds come to worship, standing in the fragrant hay. She reached out a finger and felt the tiny babe grasp it, and she knew one day her own child, Ben's babe, would cling the same way. These tranquil thoughts carried her into a deep and refreshing slumber.

CHAPTER 16

SNOW MADE IT DIFFICULT TO RECOGNIZE familiar landmarks, but Mercy had retraced the trail in her mind enough times that, even though the route was distorted under banks of white, she knew she was close to Ben's cabin. While the snow wasn't unusually deep, it was difficult to negotiate, and to cover such a distance proved more tiring than she had imagined. Not wanting to arrive exhausted, she sat down to rest a minute in the brilliant December sunshine before plunging the final distance through the shaded forest. She hadn't let herself think about Ben's reception, but now she was so near she began wondering if she'd been wise, considering his behavior when they'd parted.

"Too late, Mercy," she said aloud. "You've cast your lot. If he doesn't want you, you'll have to find someone who does." She'd already inquired concerning housekeeping work and tutoring. There was a demand for both back east, she knew. With a scarf tied over the mobcap, the scar remained acceptably hidden, and she had kept enough money from her small inheritance to take her to Philadelphia and keep her until she found a position. But that wasn't what she wanted. She wanted Ben. Sighing heavily, she picked up her case and started on. Even though she had left before daylight, it was after noon before she spotted wisps of smoke curling from the cabin standing exposed in the naked clearing.

At first, she was tempted to warn him of her arrival with the usual wilderness "Halloo," but she thought better of it and plodded unheralded to the door. After carefully brushing the snow from her boots and skirt, she drew a deep breath and knocked firmly. Inside, there was silence. She knocked again, and this time she could hear the squeak of the rocking chair and footsteps heavy on the dirt floor. Her heart pulsed frantically, and she beat down a nearly overwhelming urge to run.

Then Ben was flinging open the door, and she was looking into the muzzle of his Kentucky rifle, cradled in one arm and pointed directly at her head. She stifled a scream. he stood towering over her and he glared, unsmiling, down into her face. The beard had grown back, but even so, the scars left by Old Flop Ear were partly visible. His left eye was pulled slightly out of shape and, in the healing, his mouth left twisted. His once-handsome face was disfigured beyond hiding.

She looked into his eyes. They saw again, but they held no gladness at seeing her, and she shivered under their cold penetrating glare. "Ben, it's me, Mercy," she said at last.

"I can see that," he said, his voice a snarl as cruel and twisted as his face.

Completely unnerved, she fervently wished she'd never come. Why had she thought he would be glad to see her? *You know why,* she told herself. *Because in your heart you didn't believe him when he said he didn't need you nor want you here. It's shocking to learn he meant it.*

He kept the gun pointed at her and made no move to invite her inside. It was obvious, for all he cared, that she could turn around and go back where she'd come from. Well, she wasn't leaving without a fight.

She drew herself to her full height and thrust her case at him. "Here! I've nowhere to go. It's Christmas Day and I don't intend for you to spend it alone."

Her act so startled him that when she moved to push past him, he offered no resistance and stepped back, allowing her to enter the room.

"Oh!" she exclaimed when her eyes had adjusted to the dim interior. The place was a mess, so unlike the neat orderly cabin she'd first stepped into last fall. "What have you been doing, sharing your quarters with pigs?" she asked curtly.

Still, he said nothing.

She took off her cape and laid it over a chair. The room was chilly. Only a small fire burned the nearly consumed backlog, and there was no spare wood in the room. There were but a few small logs where there had been an abundant stack earlier. She rolled up her sleeves and built up the fire. Looking about, she located the pot for hot water lying on its side, abandoned in a corner. Bringing it to the water bucket, she discovered there was no water.

"I can't begin to fix Christmas dinner until this place is cleaned up." She shoved the empty bucket at him. "Put down that silly gun and go get some water," she ordered in a voice which brooked no nonsense.

Mercy's unexpected authority jarred Ben from his lethargy. He dropped the bucket on the floor and it rolled under the table. "I'm not going to get water, and you're not going to fix dinner. Who do you think you are, bursting into a man's cabin and ordering him about?" His roar was reminiscent of Old Flop Ear.

She turned to jelly inside. He was absolutely right. She had invaded his privacy, uninvited, and was clearly unwanted. Still, it was Christmas, and it was meant to be shared.

Defiantly, she grabbed a chair and plunked it down in front of him. She climbed up and stood a bit above eye level. Placing her hands on her hips, she shouted, "You listen here, Ben Tasker! I've come to celebrate Christmas with you, and celebrate I will, like it or not. You've turned into a crochety old he-bear living out here all alone. Now take that bucket and bring me some water. Then go get in another backlog and some more wood."

He made the mistake of looking her in the eye. *Bless Old Flop Ear*, she thought as she fixed her stare and returned glare for glare. *If I could outlast that old rogue, I surely can outstare you, Ben Tasker.*

She jumped from the chair and began jerking at the tangle of quilts on the bed. With the click of the latch, she looked over her shoulder. The room was empty. She smiled and began humming a little tune as she swept out the wood storage spot to make way for a new supply.

Presently Ben came back with the water and slammed the bucket on the table. Water sloshed over and onto the floor, leaving a dark stain on the dirt. Again, the door banged closed and she watched him stomp across the clearing, axe thrust over his shoulder. This time he returned with several armloads of wood, deposited them on the dwindling stack, and set a backlog into place in front of the fireplace, ready to be rolled in when needed.

He gave her a glare designed to produce frostbite, put on his heavy coat and a beaver cap, picked up his gun, and left. She watched him disappear into the woods. *My, but he is a stubborn one. Maybe more stubborn than I,* she thought dolefully. Although beginning to have some serious doubts about the wisdom of her coming, she had no choice now but to stay.

She worked feverishly and by midafternoon, the cabin shone. Mercy even went into the woods, cut some evergreen branches, and designed them into a spray which she hung over the fireplace. The freshly cut greenery scented the room with pine, and she smiled as she surveyed the arrangement gaily bedecked with red ribbon.

"There! The place looks better," she said aloud, and felt foolish for talking to herself.

She looked about for something to prepare for supper, but all she found was a hard crust of bread. *Maybe there's something in the springhouse.* Slipping into her cloak, she set out in the general direction she knew it to be, but the trail was snowed over. Quickly, she concluded he hadn't been using the springhouse. What had he been eating?

Back inside, she located the flour, but where did he keep the milk and butter in the winter? Not knowing what else to do, she put a pot with water on to heat. Maybe she could find something to make into soup. Then, having exhausted her resources, she picked up the broom and swept up imaginary traces of bark dropped from carrying in the wood. Finished, she stood staring into the fire. This day surely wasn't turning out as she had planned. She hadn't counted on Ben being so bitter or so stubborn. If he came back and didn't throw her out before, she'd leave first thing in the morning. If she returned to the settlement before Daniel and the family came home and found she'd gone to Ben's again, she could continue to stay with them until the weather broke and she put her other plan into action.

All the while her mind churned out these thoughts, her heart grew heavier and heavier until it lay like a stone in her breast. She did love Ben, all the more now that he was needful, and she didn't want to leave him. If only there were some way to break through the barrier he had erected so high and forebidding.

Resting her head against the broom she still held, she sighed deeply.

The stamping of feet outside broke through her reverie. Ben was back! Quickly, setting the broom in its place, she scurried about the room, uncertain what he should find her doing. A thudding knock on the door saved her from further worry. She rushed to unlatch and open it. Ben stood, filling the doorway, his gun in one hand and a fat wild turkey in the other, skinned and ready for the spit.

"Oh, Ben, what a perfect dinner he'll make!" she exclaimed, and extended her hand to take the bird.

Without speaking, Ben retained control of his kill and stepped past her into the cabin. After carefully returning the gun to its rack over the fireplace, he laid the turkey on the table and set about preparing it for cooking.

Mercy felt completely shut-out and her former boldness wilted. *Mercy, if you want this man, you're going to have to go through with what you've started. If you fail, tomorrow will be time enough to become resigned to it.*

Softly she shut the door and walked over to the table where he was skillfully skewering the bird. "I'd like to make some pies and corncakes. If you'd tell me where you've moved your supplies, I can get started.

He pointed upwards with his knife. Looking, she saw rows of tins along a shelf in the rafters, completely out of reach. She wanted to ask him to get the things for her, but something warned her to be patient a minute longer. He carried the spit to the fireplace and attached it in place, then as silently, gathered several tins from the high shelf and set them on the floor next to the table.

Mercy spun into action, cleaning off the work space. While she set out bowls and spoons, he disappeared out the door to return shortly with his arms full of milk, butter, mincemeat, sweet potatoes, and shortening.

And so it went. She chatted with him about the settlement, the family, all the news she could think of and, without speaking a word, he helped her prepare the dinner. However, she felt no animosity radiate from him. This gave her hope that in time whatever prevented him from speaking to her would disappear.

She had no lovely linen or table settings, but the dinner they sat down to would have done the finest house credit. "Would you ask the blessing, please?" she asked and folded her hands. It was hard to keep back the tears at this, the first occasion she had ever presided over a dinner table.

He cleared his throat and folded his hands. "Lord, for what we are about to eat, we give thanks."

He paused, but Mercy sensed he wasn't finished, so she kept her head bowed and waited.

"Your bounty sustains us, Lord. Your Son, whose birthday we celebrate today, has given us a path to follow. May we always see that our thoughts and actions are in keeping with the directions He provided us, so that we might return to You someday. Amen."

She looked through the flickering flames of the candles, across the small table, and into Ben's eyes. "Thank you for the lovely prayer."

While they ate in silence, a tiny glow of hope began in her heart. It continued to grow during the meal until the whole cabin felt charged with peace and love. He helped clear away dishes and then, from under his bed, he brought out a big roll of bright red felt. She helped him move the table back from the fireplace and watched as he unrolled and spread the large black fur on the floor. She smiled as she recognized Old Flop Ear's hide turned into an elegant bearskin rug.

"I lied when I said I didn't need you or want you here," he said at last.

"I know." She wanted to say more, but it was too soon. Instead, she knelt down and ran her hand over the soft luxurious fur. "Did you make this?" She turned her beaming face to his.

179

Ben stretched out on it and nodded. "Like it?"

"You've done a beautiful job. Far and away the best I've ever seen."

"When Daniel brought me the hide, he said the old rogue didn't have enough fat on him to hibernate. He'd have starved or the wolves would have gotten him. That's what made him such a dangerous beast. You really did the old boy a favor."

His familiar voice, deep, rich and musical, the words soft-stroked like velvet, washed over her. This was her Ben, back from wherever he'd been and well worth waiting for. "This dear old bear did far more for me."

He laughed, low and soft. "That wasn't the way you felt the last time you met him."

"Don't remind me. I hope never to be that frightened again."

Silently, they watched the dancing flames of the firelight, letting the early dark of winter fill the cabin. Finally, he sat up and turned to gaze fondly at her. No man had ever looked at Mercy that way and it set her quivering inside. She was torn between running in panic and throwing herself into his arms. Because the two emotions conflicted so violently, she sat quietly and did nothing.

He ran the backs of his fingers leisurely, tenderly, down the right side of her face while she turned toward the dancing flames, too timid to look at him. Then, gently pulling the bow the scarf made under her chin, he untied it and let it fall to the rug. Mercy curled the fingers of her left hand and clamped them into a fist to prevent their nearly automatic response to protect the scar. He cupped her face and drew her around until he looked full on her. Carefully, he removed the mobcap and allowed shining ebony locks to tumble down and curl about her shoulders.

She held her breath, for she knew the uncovered scar loomed, darkly blotched and ugly. She watched his eyes for a sign of revulsion. Saw nothing. Felt his thumb revolve gradually over the rough ridged surface until he completely circled the area. Trembling, she breathed again. He hadn't been repulsed by the deformity.

He caressed the left side of her face, laced long graceful fingers through her hair, then drew her to him until her head rested on his shoulder. "Tell me how you came by this." Low and soft, his voice invited her confidence.

"On a fall day when I was fourteen, I was helping my mother make soap. Daniel brought up another load of wood. I didn't hear him coming, and I backed into his path. He shoved me out of his way, but the shove was harder than he meant for it to be. I tripped and fell into the fire." How easy the telling was. For the first time, there was no anger, no blame, no hurt—nothing. She could scarcely believe it.

"And in seconds that perfect face became marred for life. At fourteen, you must have suffered agonies from more than the pain."

"Oh, I did. I refused to forgive Daniel for years, but as the years passed, I gradually came to realize, even at that young age, I was already growing vain about my looks. I was on the way to becoming a shallow, conceited person. As I thought about it later, I believe it was the Lord's way of protecting me from myself. Daniel was only a tool. He's carried a terrible load of guilt all these years, and he allows nothing I say to lighten it."

"Poor Daniel. If I'm having trouble understanding the lady who arrived on my doorstep a few hours ago, you must be driving him nearly wild. You aren't the Mercy I knew," he said.

"The Mercy everyone knew died with Old Flop Ear. No, actually I began feeling different after Esther disappeared, and I couldn't pretend she was my little girl to mother when I wanted diversion. All those

181

years, sitting unobtrusively in the corner being pious, showed up for what they were—self-imposed martyrdom and self-centered pity. I talked of God and prayed, but my prayers were only words. I didn't invest anything of myself into them. I wanted God to make my life right, but I wasn't willing to put forth any faith or take any action. Not a pretty picture when I saw what I really was—a pious fraud."

He didn't reply immediately, but turned from her and sat, a shadowy shape against the background of the fire, staring thoughtfully into the crackling flames. He seemed to have forgotten she was there, but she didn't mind. The comfort of sitting here with him, talking with him as she had heard Norah do with Daniel, was what she'd dreamed of. How good God was, giving her another chance to be with Ben. Even if this was her final time, she'd have wonderful warm memories to hold in her heart.

He smelled so clean, a piney woodsy aroma, fresh and vibrant. She ached to touch him, run her hand up over his back and around his shoulder. Did she dare? She remembered well how he looked under the shirt. The shirt! He was wearing the red shirt Genny made for him. He'd had it on when Mercy arrived. He had dressed for Christmas. Had he expected her? Just as she raised her hand to touch him, he turned.

"You've been very honest with me. I have some confessions to make, too," he said, looking deep into her eyes.

Mercy's years in the shadows had taught her one thing. She learned to listen very well, but no one had ever made her the center of conversation before. This was another new experience. Ben took her hand.

"I owe you an apology for being so rude when you arrived." He pulled at the shirt slightly and looked at it a minute before continuing. "I put on this shirt and was sitting in my chair here in front of the fireplace, feeling terribly sorry for myself. Poor Ben! His face and shoulder all scarred, his left arm weak, and worst of all, everyone he loved gone. When you knocked, I knew it was you and I was angry."

"I don't understand. If you knew it was I and you didn't want me to come in, all you had to do was refuse to open the door."

He laughed. "I was angry because I wanted you. Wanted to see you, touch you, smell the lovely fragrance of you, hear your gentle lilting voice, taste your sweet lips, feel the warmth of you—wanted it all again the way it was in the woods and by the river. Wanted it so desperately I ached with the longing." He paused and pulled her into his arms. "But I kept feeling I was betraying Genny and my children if I loved you. One minute I wanted to shout vicious accusations at you and the next, whisper tender confidences in your ear. I walked a long way for that turkey. Far enough to get my thinking straightened out."

He gathered her face between his palms, wove his fingers into her hair, and drew her to his waiting lips. Never in her wildest imagination had she dreamed of anything so sweet, for this time it was she he was kissing—wholly, passionately, possessively. So this was why Norah would give up everything, follow Daniel to the ends of the earth, and not look back.

"I love you, Mercy Wheeler, as completely and fully as I ever did Genny. The heart's a curious thing, isn't it? I don't love Genny less, but there's plenty of room there for loving you, too."

She watched the flickering light play across his face, drank deep of love flowing from dark, lustrous eyes. "Oh, Ben," she sighed at last. "I've prayed to hear those words—imagined them said in all sorts of places and in all kinds of ways, but never came close to knowing how it would really be." She tucked her fingers into his black curls and pulled his lips to hers once more, felt the tantalizing tickle of his beard, let the heady sensations sear through her.

She curled tight against his quivering body, trailed her fingers over his cheek, down his beard, and smoothed the collar of his shirt, buying time until her voice steadied. "I started loving you when you sat at my feet at the ferry landing. I knew it would never come to anything, but you made wonderful daydreams." She smiled. "Last fall after Daniel carted me away so unceremoniously, and in spite of your telling me you didn't need or want me, I made up my mind to come back here for Christmas if you didn't come to me."

He caught her fingers and stretched her hand in his, palm to palm. They smiled at each other over the comparison. His eyes glistened when he spoke. "I thought about you nearly every waking minute since you left," he said quietly. "My eyesight improved daily until the right eye came back good as ever. The left's passable. After I could see, I fought urges daily to go find you. The only thing that kept me away was those cruel words I spoke at our parting. I couldn't imagine you would want to see me. Finally, though, even that wasn't enough to keep me from you. If you hadn't arrived when you did, I'd have made up some excuse to come to the settlement. The biggest thing keeping me away was my twisted face. I couldn't think of a way to conceal my scars as you did yours, and I didn't want to frighten people."

She ran her fingers lightly over the very obvious angry red gouges. "You're much too sensitive about the scars. They aren't as bad as you imagine, but you haven't had them long enough to know that."

"Spoken by someone who really knows. I shall profit by your experience and wisdom." He hugged her. "Oh, Mercy, I do love you so."

The smile he flashed sent her heart bounding completely out of control. "And I love you, truly and forever," she whispered.

He kissed the tip of her tiny perfectly sculpted nose

and bounded to his feet. "I have something for you," he said, walking to a packing box and returning with his hand hidden behind his back. As he handed the small package to her, he said, "A small Christmas present, but there's a great deal of loving thought in it."

It was wrapped in simple white tissue. "Where did you get paper way out here?" she asked, and ran her fingers slowly over the small flat surface, prolonging the ecstasy of the surprise.

Ben rested on his haunches beside her. "That wily old peddlar doesn't miss a cabin if he can help it."

Carefully, she untied the delicate pink ribbon and unfolded the tissue. "Oh Ben," was all she could say. Tears blurred the picture he had painted of her, a small portrait framed in lacy gold showing her perfect profile. "It's lovely," she whispered and rising to her knees, she kissed him until they both gasped for breath.

"It doesn't do you justice, but after I've practiced a few years, I should do better." He paused and searched her face. "You will marry me, won't you?"

"Those were my plans, Ben Tasker." Then, added, "If you want me."

"I want you," he whispered as he held her close and kissed her with a kiss full of promises.

"I have a gift for you, too," she said when she could speak.

Returning from her case, she held out her own tissue-wrapped package and placed it in his waiting hands. She watched him untie the ribbon and open the paper as carefully as she. Smiles wreathed his face as he held up the bright blue homespun shirt Mercy had made for him. He took a long time inspecting the stitches and the cut. When he finally looked at her, his eyes were brimming with tears and he had no voice. He only shook his head and gathered her into his arms.

They clung together, wrapped in their love, until Ben broke the silence. "I'd like for us to go farther west together. I don't want you ever to feel again that you must cover that beautiful face. You can slip your hand from the cruel grip of civilization—travel without the baggage or encumbrances of the past. Out west we can start over again. Become our own higher selves, uniquely new and wonderful. Wear our scars as the badges of courage they are and never be ashamed or have to explain."

She looked into the strong face of the man she loved. "Ben Tasker, I'll travel with you wherever you want. Share your griefs and divide the joys."

ABOUT THE AUTHOR

MARYN LANGER is a delightful lady, crammed with creativity! So full of fancy and tall tales is she that one would never suspect she spends her days teaching math to classrooms of kids, nor that she has written textbooks in her chosen field. She confesses, however, that her mind, whether asleep or awake, cannot help creating wonderful characters from the past, whose lives reflect her own strong Christian faith and fortitude.

Mrs. Langer resides with her family in Albion, Idaho. A sequel to *Divide the Joy* will continue Esther's story.

A Letter to Our Readers

Dear Reader:

Welcome to the world of Serenade Books—a series designed to bring you the most beautiful love stories in the world of inspirational romance. They will uplift you, encourage you, and provide hours of wholesome entertainment, so thousands of readers have testified. In order that we might better contribute to your reading enjoyment, we would appreciate your taking a few minutes to respond to the following questions and return to:

Editor, Serenade Books
The Zondervan Publishing House
1415 Lake Drive, S.E.
Grand Rapids, Michigan 49506

1. Did you enjoy reading DIVIDE THE JOY?

☐ Very much. I would like to see more books by this author!
☐ Moderately
☐ I would have enjoyed it more if _____

_____

2. Where did you purchase this book? _____

3. What influenced your decision to purchase this book?

☐ Cover   ☐ Back cover copy
☐ Title   ☐ Friends
☐ Publicity   ☐ Other _____

4. What are some inspirational themes you would like to see treated in future books?

_____

5. Please indicate your age range:
   ☐ Under 18   ☐ 25–34   ☐ 46–55
   ☐ 18–24   ☐ 35–45   ☐ Over 55

6. If you are interested in receiving information about our Serenade Home Reader Service, in which you will be offered new and exciting novels on a regular basis, please give us your name and address. (This does NOT obligate you for membership.)

   Name _____

   Occupation _____

   Address _____

   City _____ State _____ Zip _____